The Honorable Governess

False Rumors

Laura A. Barnes

Book Cover by Laura A. Barnes

Editor: Telltail Editing

First edition 2025

To Paula

It's not very often you meet someone who shares the same sense of humor as you & relates to your quirkiness. But you are that person to me. You are an amazing soul whose friendship means the world to me. Thank you for being my friend & understanding me. To many more laughs!

The Honorable Governess

False Rumors

Chapter One

False Rumors

Sara Abbott pressed her hand against her middle as she stared at the bride before her. For the past hour, she'd denied that the reflection in the mirror was the future Duchess of Somerville. A fanciful dream she'd indulged in during her loneliness but one she'd never fathomed would ever come true. Now faced with the reality of the situation, she must accept fate's calling. While her insecurities urged her to flee, her heart begged her to remain. With every doubt rising to the surface, a whispered assurance convinced her to say "I do" when she spoke her vows.

A warm blush spread across Sara's cheeks at what awaited her once she left her bedchamber. The Duke of Somerville would become her husband. He'd become her protector from an unknown threat the past few months.

And after this evening, he could become her lover.

They hadn't even shared a kiss. The thought of sharing a bed should unsettle her innocent soul. However, she remembered his warm embrace when he comforted her during a frightful incident a month ago, and her body shivered with anticipation. His lingering touches and the intensity of his stares left Sara with no doubt that their attraction wasn't one-sided. However, she worried he wasn't as enamored of her as she was of him. To Sara, the sun rose and set with Ian Somerville. Most people would comment how unladylike it was for her to idolize Somerville as a hero, but he held the characteristics of a gentleman who possessed not a single flaw of imperfection.

While she hoped their wedding resulted from Somerville professing his undying love for her, the reality was that he only offered marriage to protect her from a threat that had escalated since they arrived in London. They had traveled to London for the holiday season to visit Somerville's late wife's family, the Whethams. He wanted his daughter, Mairi, to remain close to her grandparents. However, their visit had spoiled once rumors spread of Sara's involvement with the duke. Every rumor rang false, but it had garnered enough attention for the ton to question Somerville's standing as an honorable duke among his peers.

When she attempted to flee, Lady Whetham had stopped her by convincing Sara that her departure would harm Mairi. She feared Mairi would retreat into her shell again. Since Sara arrived in Mairi's life, the young girl had blossomed under Sara's attention. Not only Mairi but her father too. While the lady still grieved over her daughter's death, she recognized how Somerville and her granddaughter cared for Sara. Lady Whetham considered Sara to be the key to Somerville's and Mairi's happiness.

Lord and Lady Whetham's kindness had overwhelmed Sara when she first arrived. Other than Somerville, Sara had been unaccustomed to friendliness from the aristocracy. Except her friends, who had become members of the peerage with their marriages. However, the employers of her past had treated her with disregard or else they'd attempted to accost her. Memories she hoped to escape from but they still kept a tight hold on her existence.

A knock against the door ended Sara's reflection. She didn't want to tarnish Somerville's pristine image by him marrying his governess, but there were no other options before her. She was alone in this world, besides her three friends, and she refused to become a burden to them. Especially since they lived full lives with their own families. With no family to turn to, she welcomed the chance to become Mairi's mother. She made a solemn vow to make Ian proud of her and never regret his offer.

Vivian Courtland peeked her head around the door. "I heard you are in need of a friend."

Sara gasped and swirled around at her friend's voice. "You came."

Vivian rushed to Sara's side. "Of course, dear heart. I would not have missed your wedding for the world."

Sara's lips trembled as she fought to keep her tears from falling. She thought she was alone in the world. However, Ian had already proven himself worthy of her affections by seeing to the comforting warmth of her friendships. Vivian's arrival was proof of his devotion to her. While she wanted nothing more than to become his wife, her doubts about her status as his governess kept her rooted in her bedchamber. Sara hoped Vivian would help her see reason and calm her insecurities.

Vivian brushed her thumb under Sara's eye, capturing a tear. "Today is for smiles, no tears." She held her arms open for Sara.

Sara fell into Vivian's embrace and whispered, "This is a mistake."

Vivian led Sara to the settee near the fireplace. "A blessing, I believe."

Sara lifted her head off Vivian's shoulder. "A blessing?"

Vivian nodded.

"Not for everyone involved. For myself, yes. This marriage will offer me the security I have never held. However, the marriage for the duke will only bring shame upon him and his daughter."

"You speak utter nonsense," Vivian denied.

Sara sighed. "I wish I do. However, I only speak the truth."

"Is this the reason you hide?"

Sara pinched her lips and stayed silent.

Vivian brushed her hand down Sara's head in a comforting caress. It reminded Sara of how her grandmother used to comfort her, which brought forth another ache of sadness. Sara wished her grandmother were alive to see her marry the gentleman of her dreams. Nana would've known the exact words to quiet Sara's nerves. She missed her grandmother something fierce. Her entire life, the lady had offered Sara her love and guidance, even though it had been a struggle to raise her. She'd never once made Sara feel as if she were a burden. While Somerville never expressed he considered marrying her to be, Sara thought differently. She refused to be a burden to anyone, like she was to her parents.

"I wish you could see yourself as others do," Vivian continued when Sara never responded. "You are the sweetest soul I have the fortune of calling a friend. If Grace and Flora were here, they would agree. Your gentle guidance over the past year helped us to overcome our difficulties and urged us not to deny the love within our grasp. It is my greatest honor to offer you that wisdom now. Somerville is smitten with you, my friend, and his daughter has thrived under your care. You are the missing piece to their family. Do not deny them or yourself this happiness."

"His offer of marriage is but a noble gesture. I do not wish to be a burden."

Vivian chuckled. "Oh, Sara. Somerville's offer is anything but noble. You are far from a burden to him."

Sara's eyebrows pinched together. "I do not understand."

Vivian smiled at her friend with patience. Sara's innocence made her the perfect bride for the Duke of Somerville. She only hoped the duke didn't wait too long before confessing the depth of his love for Sara. Her friend remained in a fragile state, with the threats to her safety escalating. She needed reassurance more than anything.

Vivian gathered Sara's hands in hers. "Somerville's offer of marriage was inevitable. He is a gentleman who desires you and would have eventually offered for your hand. Somerville would never have tarnished your virtue for his own pleasure."

Sara blushed at what Vivian implied. "But he has attempted no untoward advances."

"Nor would he. He values your innocence and does not want you to view him in the same light as his other peers."

"Lord Baldridge."

Vivian squeezed Sara's hands. "Aye."

Lord Baldridge, Sara's former employer, was an earl who'd attempted to seduce her with his wife in the next room. While she had enjoyed caring for his children, he'd made her employment uncomfortable. She'd confided her dilemma to her friends, and they had retaliated by seeking their revenge against the lord at a ball. They embarrassed Lord Baldridge with their truth and Vivian's act of pulling his hairpiece off his head. However, their act of revenge only ruined them. Lord Baldridge kept his rankings in the peerage, while Sara and her friends were dismissed and shunned from ever finding employment in England. A scandalous rumor resulted in defending her honor, one that had left them desolate.

With Vivian's determination, she'd secured their positions in Scotland. As a result, Vivian, Grace, and Flora had found their happily ever after. Sara found much joy in their happiness. However, she was realistic enough to understand she'd never be so lucky to find the same bliss. It was only fanciful dreams she envisioned where the duke declared his love for her. Never in her wildest fantasies had she ever imagined she would become his bride.

"The rumor started again."

"Somerville explained in his letter."

Sara attempted a smile. "While I am comforted by your arrival, you did not need to travel to London for my sake."

"We had just arrived in London to visit Maximilian's family when we received word from Somerville. So it is no hardship but an honor to join in your celebration. Is Mairi excited you will be her new mama?" Vivian asked.

Sara's smile widened. "She has been a bundle of energy ever since we told her."

Vivian laughed. "Oh, that warms my heart to hear. And the Whethams?"

"They express their happiness with the union and have welcomed me into their family as if I were one of their own."

Vivian stood and held out her hands. "Then there is no reason to delay any longer."

Sara allowed Vivian to help her rise and guide her toward the door. While Sara could name a hundred different reasons to stall, only her insecurities kept her from walking down the stairs and becoming the Duchess of Somerville. Because for every reason to delay, she also held every reason to marry Ian. And they far outweighed her doubts.

From this day forth, Sara vowed she would bring no shame upon Somerville and Mairi. She would devote herself to their happiness. Because once she spoke her vows, she would find so much joy in becoming a family with them. Any doubts about their marriage would vanish once Somerville fell in love with her the way she loved him.

Sara hugged Vivian. “Thank you for helping me see reason.”

Vivian returned the hug. “’Tis what friends are for.”

Sara had never been alone at all.

False Rumors

Somerville paced back and forth across his father-in-law’s study as he waited for Sara to join them. He feared he’d pressured Sara into marrying him with his abrupt proposal. He played upon her vulnerability to keep her protected because of her limited options, but his only reason was that he refused to wait another day to marry her. His urgency only proved the rumors to hold the truth, even though they were far from it. His only intimacy with his governess was when he’d comforted her from a fright in a roomful of their closest friends. However, none of them would dare betray him or Sara. All of them had proven their loyalty and would protect Sara to the end if necessary.

Sara awakened his soul again when he held her in his embrace. Since she’d arrived at his home to govern his daughter, he had denied his feelings and fought his attraction to her. When he learned of the ordeal of her last employer’s transgressions, he’d refused to make her uncomfortable by any means. Instead, he'd held his admiration in check while she cared for Mairi. But after holding her soft curves against him, he'd realized he could no longer refuse what his heart wanted. Was he a selfish bastard by convincing Sara to marry him? Aye. But he refused to bend. Especially when he wanted to protect her and offer her the family she deserved.

Mairi loved Sara as a mother. Sara's devotion to his daughter only endeared her to him even more. Before she arrived, Mairi had found no joy in life but suffered every day from her sorrows. The governesses before Sara had never allowed Mairi to mourn. Instead, they'd tried to force her to forget her mother. Once Sara arrived, her gentle direction had allowed Mairi to grieve and enjoy the simple acts in life again.

He could spend hours reciting every single glowing attribute about Sara, but it still wouldn't excuse his behavior. With each second of her delay in joining them for their wedding, guilt festered in his gut. His selfish needs had frightened her.

"I am no better than Lord Baldridge," Somerville muttered.

Lord Courtland scoffed. "Baldridge is gutter swine and not even considered a gentleman."

"Still, my intentions are even less honorable."

Courtland leaned back in the chair. "You cannot compare yourself to Baldridge. He only wanted to ruin Miss Abbott, where your intention is to protect her."

Somerville winced at how Courtland made him out to be Sara's hero. His obvious attention toward his governess raised many eyebrows. He was positive Courtland had noticed and was too much of a gentleman to state otherwise. His in-laws hadn't been so reluctant to state their opinion of his behavior toward his governess. In fact, they'd surprised him with how they encouraged the suit.

When they arrived for the holiday season, they had treated Sara with the proper distance they did with all of their servants. However, as the days passed, they'd noticed how Mairi blossomed under Sara's care. Soon, their own sorrows had lifted by Sara's kind gestures to keep his late wife's memory alive. Her kindhearted actions with Mairi had shown his mother-in-law how special Sara was to them. After the holiday season ended, Lady Whetham had commented on his longing glances and encouraged him to pursue Sara. His father-in-law wholeheartedly agreed. They didn't hold the strict opinion of the peerage about only associating with their station.

Somerville cleared his throat. "No need to placate me, Courtland. You are well aware I hold a tenderness for Miss Abbott."

Courtland winked and raised his glass of whiskey at Somerville. "All the more reason to make her your bride. A scandal is the last thing the miss needs. However, you acting upon your desires after you wed is between you and Miss Abbott. You are only preventing the governess's ruination by making her your duchess."

"It still does not justify my actions."

Courtland sighed, sitting forward in the chair. "Set aside the threats against Miss Abbott. What are your feelings for the lady? Would you have eventually made her your bride?"

Somerville strode to the bar cart and poured himself a whiskey. He had refrained from any spirits until now because of his need to keep a clear head. However, his doubts soared and crashed with regret for pushing her into a marriage she may not have wanted. Perhaps he was mistaken about the tender gazes she bestowed upon him when she thought he wasn't aware. Was he forcing her into a commitment she wanted to share with somebody else?

He threw back the shot in one swallow. Courtland's all-knowing stare stayed fixated on him as he waited for an answer. Somerville poured another drink as a delay tactic. It was a harsh admittance but one most obvious because of the difference in their ranks in society. He was a duke who employed Sara as his governess. It didn't matter how his heart had ached for more the past few months. In truth, if there were never any threats against Sara and the rumors of an illicit affair between them hadn't spread through the ton's gossip vine, he never would've offered her marriage.

Courtland grabbed the drink from Somerville's hand and poured it out into a nearby plant. "Let us keep our wits about us. Aye?"

Somerville swiped his hand down his face. "Aye." He took up his pacing again to calm his nerves. "I care about Miss Abbott deeply. However, threats and rumors aside, I doubt if I would have offered for her hand. My status in society would never allow me the freedom."

He paused at the gasp echoing around them. When he turned toward the doorway, he saw Sara hovering over the threshold with her arms wrapped around her middle. She opened her mouth and then closed it again. With tears in her eyes, she turned and fled.

"Sara," Somerville croaked.

He ran after her, only for Lady Courtland to stand in his way. She held out her hand. "Give her a moment to compose herself."

Somerville growled. "Please step aside."

Courtland stepped to his wife's side to further block Somerville. "Allow Miss Abbott a few minutes to herself before you follow her."

"But ..."

Lady Courtland placed her hand on Somerville's sleeve. "She will not run."

Sommerville stared at the emptiness behind the Courtlands. He'd lost her. Not physically but emotionally. Whatever he would say to her, she would never believe him. She'd overheard the truth, and no matter what feelings they held for each other, his honesty had set them on a path of disappointment.

Disappointment they could hopefully overcome as long as regret never settled between them.

Chapter Two

False Rumors

Sara ran to the garden to escape the humiliation of Somerville's confession. His conversation with Lord Courtland proved she was but a burden he'd rescued in his attempt to be her knight in shining armor. His intentions might be honorable, but her heart broke to learn the truth of how he felt about her.

She swiped at her tears as she settled on a bench tucked away behind a thicket of bushes. She had discovered the hiding space on the second day of their visit. Sara had always felt uncomfortable around the aristocracy, and the Whethams' warm welcoming confused her. Their behavior didn't differ from her friends. However, she was unaccustomed to their kind treatment. Servants were to perform their duties in the background, not enjoy tea with the lady of the manor as if they were friendly acquaintances. How was she to grace everyone with a smile of happiness that she was marrying the gentleman of her dreams when it was all false?

Sara had never felt more alone. Even with Vivian's support, it didn't strip away the sense that she didn't belong in their world. She missed the simple life she had shared with her grandmother. Perhaps the villain's suggestion of returning to Fordwich was her only option.

She had fooled herself into believing Somerville had fallen in love with her by his ardent attention of late. He had been so protective and had comforted her when the villain's threats frightened her. She had mistaken his kind gestures for acts of affection. How naïve she had been. Now she must make a decision that would only end in heartache.

If she left, it would break her heart to part from Mairi and Somerville, and she would be left with no prospects for employment. As for a home, she could return to her grandmother's cottage. It'd been impossible to part with the place after her death. However, if she stayed, she would enter a loveless marriage. To spend a lifetime married to a gentleman who never returned her love would be devastating. Somerville would always consider her an obligation. Could she marry Somerville under those circumstances?

A handkerchief floated down onto Sara's lap. She glanced up to meet Somerville's guilt-stricken gaze. She lowered her head and curled her fingers around the linen. It was foolish, but she felt his warmth seep onto her fingertips from the cloth.

"This spot used to be Claudia's favorite place to sneak away to," Somerville reminisced.

Sara gasped, horrified at invading a sacred place for Somerville, and attempted to rise. "I apologize."

Somerville reached out to stop Sara from leaving. "I am glad you find the same comfort here."

Sara wiped away her tears and held the handkerchief out to return to Somerville, but he shook his head in response. She stayed silent, unsure how to respond to him and the awkwardness they now faced since she'd discovered his true feelings for her.

Somerville leaned back to rest against the bench and stared at Sara. The silence between them might seem uncomfortable, yet he found it to be soothing and took great comfort in it. She was lovely to gaze upon, with her honey curls flowing around her shoulders. The white gown she wore for their wedding hugged her petite frame. He wished she would meet his eyes so he could lose himself in their aqua depths. However, he had blundered his chance with his callous remarks.

A chilly wind swept by, causing Sara to shiver. Now he was an insensitive brute. While he sat admiring her, Sara froze in her thin attire. He swore silently under his breath so as not to cause her any more distress. He rose, tore off his suit coat, and swept it across her shoulders. Somerville sat back down and gathered her hands into his. She stiffened but soon softened at his intimate touch. He attempted to focus on soothing her troubled thoughts. However, touching her overwhelmed his senses. He had lied to Courtland about how he never would've asked for Sara's hand in marriage. It was the response his fellow peer expected to hear. But in truth, ever since Sara entered his life, he had thought of nothing else. He grew tired of denying his feelings for the girl. He only hoped Sara would grant him her forgiveness.

"Are you warm enough?" At Sara's nod, Somerville continued. "I want to apologize for what you overheard."

"'Tis unnecessary," Sara murmured.

"I never meant a word I spoke to Lord Courtland."

"Please do not deny your true feelings," Sara whispered.

"'Tis not how I truly feel. Those are the words of a pretentious duke speaking to his fellow peer. Not of a duke who has fallen for his governess."

Sara withdrew her hand from Somerville's grasp. "There is no need for you to sweeten your words, Your Grace. I have already promised I will marry you. Even though our marriage will bring shame to your good family name, I will not tarnish it by leaving you alone at the altar."

Somerville curled in his fingers to keep from reaching for Sara again. Her withdrawal bothered him more than he cared to admit. He feared his feelings ran deeper for Sara than those he'd shared with his late wife. Claudia's death had devastated him, and he'd sworn never to love with that intensity again.

However, the passion that consumed him whenever he was near Sara showed he was setting himself up for the same heartache, or worse, if something would ever happen to Sara. Already, the threats against her brought out his protective instincts to offer her marriage.

It wouldn't matter how he responded to Sara. She was determined to believe his lies. He had placed himself in a real quandary with his pretentious remarks. He hadn't realized his sweet-natured governess could be so stubborn. Just another endearing quality he could admire. He would bide his time and show her how much she meant to him after the ceremony.

Somerville rose and offered his hand to help Sara rise. "Very well then. Shall we not keep our guests waiting?"

Sara placed her hand in his, and the all-consuming butterflies fluttered to life again from his mere touch. His patient smile overwhelmed her senses. However, she must keep herself composed and not allow him to discover how greatly he affected her. It would only make him pity her more. Even though his smile held the same kindness, the sparkle in his eyes confused her. It held a flicker of undeniable passion that had her averting her gaze. However, her curiosity got the better of her. She glanced back, only to see patience reflected in his eyes. She must've been mistaken about Somerville holding any sort of desire for her.

They walked in silence until they reached the drawing room where Lady Whetham had arranged the ceremony to take place. Soft conversation drifted into the hallway, causing Sara to pause. Before she could plead with Somerville to change his mind, Mairi ran toward them and wrapped her arms around Sara's legs.

"I thought you had left." Mairi hiccupped between a sob.

Sara knelt to draw Mairi into her arms, running her hand along her hair in a soothing gesture. "Never, my love."

Sara abandoned all arguments and doubts in the face of Mairi's reaction to her absence. She couldn't allow this sweet child to suffer any more loss in her young life. Mairi had thrived since her mother's death, coming out of her shell. When Sara met the girl, she had wanted to weep at the devastation the mite had suffered. Now the girl and her father welcomed her into their family with open arms. She finally realized she helped to make them whole.

Sara only hoped the threats against her never impacted this family. If so, then she would regret speaking her vows to Somerville.

Somerville lifted Mairi into his arms. "Miss Abbott needed a breath of fresh air."

Mairi frowned. "She is not Miss Abbott anymore, Poppa. She is Momma."

Somerville threw his head back and laughed at his daughter's correction. Leave it to his child to simplify their connection to Sara. They were doomed if his daughter couldn't tug on Sara's heartstrings with her grand declaration. He tweaked her nose. "Right you are, poppet. But only after she says I do."

Mairi reached out to touch Sara's curls. "Tell Poppa I do."

Sara smiled with fondness at Mairi before bestowing her smile on him. His breath caught at the adoration she held in her gaze. He didn't know if it was for him or for his daughter. Nor did he care at that point. Only if she continued staring at them in the same manner until the end of time.

"I do." Sara's whisper-soft declaration settled in his heart.

Mairi clapped. "Now you are my momma."

Lady Whetham stepped into the hallway. "Now to make it official." She held out her arms for Mairi and started walking away with her granddaughter. She glanced over her shoulder and focused her gaze on Sara. "Is all well?"

Sara nodded, and Lady Whetham continued inside the drawing room, leaving Sara alone with Somerville once again. Neither of them spoke. Whether from uncertainty or fear that their wishes would turn to ashes, Sara didn't know. Only for that spell, the universe granted Sara the comfort of belonging to something grander than she had ever imagined. Her life would change from this moment forward. It was her choice to make it everything she'd ever wanted it to be.

Sara rested her hand on Somerville's sleeve. "Shall we, Your Grace?"

Somerville would correct Sara later about how he expected her to address him. Preferably when they were alone and he could see her blush when she called him by his Christian name. Right before he claimed her lips in a kiss as husband and wife. For now, her acceptance of speaking their vows relieved his guilty conscience. Once he convinced Sara of his true intentions, he would confess his sins. Until then, he would protect her with his life. She would be his duchess and untouchable.

He dared anyone to defy his protection.

False Rumors

The wedding ceremony was a modest affair, involving the Courtlands and the Whethams. Mairi stood between them, holding each of their hands while they spoke their vows. Somerville spoke with a softness that held tender affection, causing Sara to fall deeper under his charming spell. She had expected him to repeat the lines with firm determination. However, he acted as if their wedding resulted from them falling in love, not him offering marriage to keep her protected. While he spoke his vows out of necessity, Sara spoke hers out of love.

The brush of his lips against her cheek once the priest announced them husband and wife still tingled. She caught herself on multiple occasions pressing her hand against the spot he'd kissed, hoping to capture the warmth and spread it into her soul. Each minute that passed since she became Ian's wife, the Duchess of Somerville, the more flustered she became. Especially when Somerville wandered near her and inquired about her welfare. His display of affection didn't go unnoticed by her or the guests in the drawing room.

The Whethams had invited a few influential members of the ton for a reception to show their support of the marriage. They wanted to leave no doubt that they accepted Sara into their family. Lady Whetham introduced Sara to the ladies as if she were her own daughter, telling them how blessed they were to have Sara join their family. She spoke her sentiments with genuine heartfelt affection, with not a trace of false malice.

"Is it still warm?" Vivian teased.

Sara blushed. Her fingers drifted away from her cheek to tuck a curl behind her ear. "Yes, it has grown warm with the arrival of more guests."

Vivian chuckled. She didn't address Sara's change of subject. Her friend had endured enough confusion for the day to add to her discomfort. However, she would impart some advice. After all, it was the least a friend could do to a newly married duchess. "I remember when Maximilian first courted me. I would lie awake for hours, reminiscing on our time spent together. Each whispered word where we shared our secrets and dreams. Each soft caress as he guided me around the dance floor. Each stolen kiss. Those moments blossomed into an unforgettable love. One that you will soon share with Somerville if you allow yourself to believe."

Sara stared at Somerville, who was speaking with his father-in-law. His deep chuckle reached them across the room. She turned toward Vivian. "Is it possible?"

Vivian's eyes twinkled. "Yes, my dear. Every dream you have ever imagined will come true if you place your faith in your husband. Because he already has with you."

Sara swung her gaze back to Somerville to see his attention focused on her. If she stared deeply into his eyes, Sara could almost believe Vivian. She turned back to her friend with a wistful smile. "Dreams are all I treasure at the moment."

Vivian wrapped Sara in a hug. "Congratulations, my friend. I will call on you before we return to Scotland."

"Thank you for your encouraging support today. I would not have survived without you."

Vivian smiled. "Nonsense. You are stronger than you believe."

Sara watched Vivian join her husband as they offered their farewells to Somerville and his in-laws. Once the Courtlands departed, the other guests spoke their goodbyes too. Sara should've moved to Somerville's side and offered her gratitude for their attendance at their wedding reception. However, she stayed behind in the shadows, unsure of her position in Somerville's life. Did he intend for her to be his wife in full regard? Or was she his wife in name only? The rush of their nuptials left Sara confused with so many unanswered questions.

Once she realized Somerville didn't need her, she slipped away and climbed the stairs to Mairi's bedchamber. Mairi had kicked off the blanket, and Sara tugged it around her tiny frame. She brushed Mairi's hair back and placed a kiss on her forehead. They had allowed her to stay awake past her bedtime to join in the festivities. Once the other guests arrived, a maid had taken Mairi away to prepare for bed. Sara had missed reading Mairi a bedtime story this evening. One she would remedy tomorrow and every night forth. Her marriage provided her a secure position in Mairi's life.

Sara sat in the rocking chair near the bed and watched over Mairi as she slept. She hoped her marriage to Somerville held no troublesome consequences for the child. She didn't want father and child to suffer because of her status in society. Her marriage might have elevated her standings, but it would never wipe away the stain of her position in their lives.

Today should've been the happiest day of her life, but Sara only held a sadness she struggled to overcome. One she must because she never wanted Somerville to regret his grand offer or for him to see she didn't appreciate everything he had ever done for her. Because she appreciated him. She only wished today's events had occurred under different circumstances, ones she had dreamed of since she was a young girl. However, they were only the fanciful dreams of a naïve miss. Not a governess's reality.

She closed her eyes and set the chair into motion. The gentle glide of the rocker helped to ease her troubled thoughts. Slowly, the tension seeped away, leaving her with a slight relief from her worries. She brought her hand back up to her cheek, hoping to capture Somerville's warmth. The memory of his affection twined its way around her heart. If only she could suspend time and lose herself in his attention focused solely on her.

Somerville leaned against the doorjamb to his daughter's bedchamber. After a loving glance at his sleeping child, he focused his attention on his wife. He'd never expected to refer to another lady with the title, but it fit Sara to perfection. The timid governess was now his. He had seen her sneak away from the reception and wished to follow her by whisking her away to his bedchamber. However, she needed time alone after the day she'd endured.

Also, he didn't want to frighten her with his eagerness for her to become his wife to the fullest meaning imaginable, an act that needed to wait while he courted her to fall in love with him. It would be a slow courtship for her to accept him as her husband and for her to realize they were a family, one he hoped to grow over the years. It had warmed his heart to find she had sneaked away to be near his daughter.

He stepped forward and winced when the floorboards creaked underneath him. Sara's eyes flew open, and she clutched at the chair handles. Once she noticed it was him, her hold loosened and her breath rushed out. She offered him a timid smile before averting her gaze. He cringed at frightening her.

"Please forgive me," Somerville whispered.

Sara rose and whispered, "There is nothing to forgive, Your Grace."

Sommerville frowned at how Sara addressed him. While he understood she found the transition from his governess to his duchess a trying ordeal, he needed to address her formality. She was under the impression he'd only married her to offer her protection and present a front of a happily married couple to trick the villain who threatened her. But when he declared his vows to her, he'd meant every word, even down to the "till death do us part." Also, he longed for her to call him Ian.

He offered his arm. "Shall we continue this conversation elsewhere, so as not to awaken Mairi?"

Sara bit at her bottom lip, unsure what else the duke wished to discuss with her this evening. She glanced at Mairi sleeping peacefully, unaware of Sara's scattered emotions. She wished to hide away in her bedchamber and escape her new reality. However, she couldn't deny the duke his simple request. Her resistance wasn't because the duke threatened her under any nature, only because she feared she'd make a fool out of herself by throwing herself at him. His brief kiss after the priest declared them husband and wife had left a resounding impact on her emotions.

She placed her hand on his arm. "Yes, Your Grace."

Sara gave Somerville a startled glance as he guided them out of Mairi's bedchamber and led them along the hallway. If she wasn't mistaken, she'd heard a soft growl from him after she agreed. However, his blank expression disputed that fact. Perhaps she was mistaken. After all, why should it bother him if she addressed him properly? She may be his wife, but that only made her respect him more.

Lost in her thoughts, she neglected to see where he led her. It wasn't until he released her hold and closed the door that Sara became aware he'd walked them to his bedchamber. When he strode past her to the bar cart in the corner, she took a hesitant step toward the door.

Somerville poured them each a glass of wine. He needed something in his grip to keep himself from drawing Sara into his arms and kissing *Your Grace* from her lips. He needed to draw on every ounce of patience he could muster or he would show his bride a new side of himself he hadn't been aware he possessed. Sara stirred emotions in him he hadn't believed himself capable of. With his first wife, he had found contentment with the gentle lovemaking they shared. However, with Sara, passion flowed through him with the need to ravish her.

He threw back the glass of wine, but it wasn't strong enough to prevent him from striding across the bedchamber and devouring Sara. With an unsteady hand, he poured himself a glass of whiskey. More than what he usually imbibed but enough to keep him centered. He drank half the glass before he turned back to his wife, who was backing toward the door with a wide stare. In his quest to calm himself, he had somehow frightened Sara. He swiped a hand along his face at his thoughtlessness. While he was a mature gentleman who understood the ways of the world, his bride held a sweet innocence of naivety.

Being alone with him in his bedchamber sent her into shock. Her hand trembled as she reached for the door handle. He had bumbled his attempt to woo her with his demanding nature of expecting everyone to fall along with his requests. It had not been his intent to make Sara uneasy when he led her into his bedchamber. He had only wished to begin his courtship. In his negligence, he hadn't considered how the scene presented itself. Sara must assume he would demand his husbandly rights, when, in fact, he only wanted to put her at ease and steal a sweet kiss from her luscious lips.

Now, to convince her his intentions were innocent at best.

Chapter Three

False Rumors

SARA GRIPPED THE DOOR handle as if her life depended on it. Her gaze darted around the suite, noticing the opulence. It was a far cry from her servant's quarters. The Whethams had given her a decorated room near Mairi, but it didn't hold the depth of their wealth as Somerville's rooms. He didn't have a simple bedchamber with a bed but multiple rooms to see to his needs. When he closed the door, it was to the sitting area, complete with chairs and a settee near the fireplace. A desk sat nestled in the corner with papers stacked in an orderly fashion.

Two other doors led to what she could only presume was a bathing area and his bedchamber. She gulped at the sight, and her imagination ran wild. What was his intention to ask her to accompany him? Did he pour them wine hoping to seduce her? The question she should ask was: should she flee? However, she already knew her answer by how she stayed rooted in place, waiting for his next move.

Somerville strode to her side with a glass of wine. "Would you mind joining me for a drink before we retire for the evening?"

Sara nodded, hypnotized by the dazzling smile he bestowed her. When he handed her the glass and their finger brushed, Sara had to bite back a sigh from his exquisite touch. She rushed past him to sit on the settee before her knees gave out from underneath her. She now understood how it was possible to swoon at a gentleman's attention. She drank a gulp of wine to keep from embarrassing herself, only to choke on the potency of the flavored brew.

Somerville took the goblet from her hand. "'Tis best to sip the wine."

Sara blushed. He must believe her to be a simpleminded village maiden and regretted tarnishing his reputation by marrying her. She bowed her head and folded her hands in her lap. It was best not to respond and allow him to lead the conversation, less she embarrassed herself more.

Somerville sighed as he placed the goblet on the table next to the settee. He took a seat next to her, because sitting across from her would defeat his intention. Also, he hoped to ease the tension between them by showing her they could be friends. However, when she stiffened next to him, he realized his every attempt today left her shyer than ever.

He lifted her chin with the soft brush of his fingers and offered her a reassuring smile. "I only thought to warn you about the wine because I noticed you do not engage in drinking spirits."

Sara fought back her tears at his kindness. She felt so overwhelmed and wanted nothing more than his warm embrace to chase her worries away. "Thank you, Your Grace, for your sincere gesture."

Somerville growled. "Ian."

Somerville's growl left Sara with little doubt that her reference to his status displeased him. "Tis not appropriate to address you with intimacy when we are still strangers to one another."

Somerville chuckled and leaned back against the cushions, amused at his wife's deference to keep a wall of unfamiliarity between them. "I believe our marriage vows today state differently."

Sara sat up straighter. "Today was only a formality. I see no reason for a change in our relationship or the position you hired me for."

"I disagree."

His husky whisper caused Sara to whip her head around to state her disagreement, only to become entranced by his seductive smile. She shook her head to clear away her wanton thoughts. Was he flirting with her? What an absurd thought. Or was it? However, as she stared into his eyes, the midnight hue flickered into a darker shade filled with yearning for a moment before transforming back into determined patience.

Sara cleared her throat. "I am unclear what you want."

Somerville groaned at her innocent statement. She held no clue how the words affected him and the hidden meaning behind them. He didn't dare state his desires at that moment. Soon, but not now. He was the one to clear his throat this time. "I wish to make you happy by becoming the best husband for you. Also, for us to spend a lifetime making memories to cherish with one another."

His answer left her speechless. Why would a gentleman of his standing want to make his governess happy? Somerville made no sense with his attention and ramblings. Perhaps he had overindulged too much today and would regret this conversation tomorrow. 'Twas best if she placated him for now, then tomorrow they could resume their lives as normal.

"And you have, Your Grace."

Somerville could blame it on the whiskey he indulged in. However, it would be a lie. Her uttering of another *Your Grace* set him on a path he would never regret.

Except for the part where he behaved as an obnoxious gentleman because of his need to kiss Sara with senseless abandonment.

He would ponder his behavior later, but for now, the sweet taste of her mouth under his left him powerless to the passion he had kept tamed since he met her.

He was a brute with how he drew her into his arms and pressed his lips against hers. Somerville fought against ravishing them with his unsuppressed need. Instead, he coaxed her mouth open with the gentle brushing of his tongue across her lips. At her sigh, she melted in his arms and clutched at his lapels as she parted her lips under his. Her reaction left him in no doubt about how his shy governess wanted to kiss him too. Nay. His wife accepted his kiss as he had always dreamed she would.

When Sara's arms crept around his neck and she sank her fingers through his hair, he deepened the kiss to draw her sweetness into his lonely soul. Their tongues tangled in a dance of slow seduction, each of them drawing their sighs into the other. He leaned back, pulling Sara with him. He wanted to clutch her to his heart for an eternity. She was the other half of his soul, and he wanted to shower her with the love she so deserved.

Sara lost herself in Somerville's kiss. She should push out of his arms, but his warmth enveloped her in a romantic cocoon she never wanted to leave. The gentle brush of his lips held a hint of untamed passion she wished he would unleash on her. She never expected the duke to show her any affection since their marriage was a farce to protect her. Another reason she should step away from his embrace because he obviously never meant to kiss her.

She savored the exotic flavor of the whiskey he drank and became light-headed at the sheer intensity of his passion. Her fingers sank into his golden tresses, and his kiss became more demanding. Because of her inexperience, she followed his lead and mimicked his actions, stroking her tongue along his and running it across his lips. His moans only encouraged her to match him kiss for kiss. When his grip tightened around her, a heady power overtook her with how she pleased the duke with her passion.

"Sara," Somerville moaned.

His husky drawl of her name brought Sara to her senses at how wanton she behaved toward Somerville. What had possessed her to lose herself in their kiss? How did the duke perceive her actions? Would he believe the rumors about her previous employment with Lord Baldridge?

She shoved against his chest for him to release her. Somerville loosened his hold, and Sara leapt to her feet, rushing behind the armchair. She tugged on her skirts and pressed her hands against her cheeks to cool them. However, they flamed with the heat overtaking her. Whether from mortification or the passion they shared coursing through her veins, she would never know. Nor did she want to ponder the answer.

"Somerville. Your Grace," Sara stumbled to explain.

Somerville folded his arms across his chest to keep from reaching for Sara. "Ian."

Sara's hand fluttered in the air. "I apologize for my forwardness."

Somerville's lips lifted in amusement, and he fought back a chuckle. "No need to on my account, my love. I quite enjoyed your response. Also, I have no intention of offering you an apology when I instigated it."

Sara's lips pinched. "An act you will regret on the morrow once you come to your senses."

"I am in complete control of my senses, sweet Sara." He rose off the settee and brushed his thumb across her lips, wanting to ease her discomfort. "I will regret nothing pertaining to you."

Sara brushed Somerville's hand away. She couldn't articulate an argument with him standing so close. She opened her mouth to make him see reason, but he lowered his head to kiss her again. Her eyelids fluttered at his intoxicating kiss. However, before he enticed her with the promise of seduction, he stepped back. Her soft moan of disappointment echoed around them.

Somerville rocked on his heels with a smile of satisfaction. Who was this gentleman impersonating the duke? This wasn't the patient employer who showed her kindness by offering her protection with a marriage of convenience. She had never seen him behave in a mischievous mood, not even with his own daughter. He always held a seriousness about him, leaving no one in doubt of his rank and power. Obviously, his overindulgence in the potent whiskey and wine he drank throughout the day had taken control of his common sense.

It was dire for her sanity to leave him for the evening. If not, she would allow him to sweep her off her feet, straight to his bed. Then they would live their married days with regret they could never disregard. That wouldn't be fair to Mairi. She must consider Mairi before she lost herself in Somerville's kisses again. No matter how much they shook her very foundation. She mustn't risk Somerville's displeasure. Two people who should've loved her had abandoned her at her most vulnerable. She couldn't handle Somerville's abandonment too.

Sara rushed to the door but stopped when Somerville spoke his next demand.

"I wish for you to call me Ian."

If he had stated that he expected her to call him Ian, she would have defied him with a list of reasons for the inappropriateness. However, now she could never deny him since he stated it was his wish.

Her heart already called him Ian.

False Rumors

Somerville strode into the breakfast room the next morning with a spring in his step he hadn't felt for quite some time. The kiss he'd shared with Sara had overshadowed every one of his worries, as if they didn't exist. Most would assume his wedding night brought forth a smile to his lips. However, he'd spent the hours alone in his bed. His bride had slept in the spare cot in his daughter's bedchamber. He could only assume once she learned the servants had moved her belongings into his suite, she'd resigned herself to sleeping with his daughter as her protector.

She didn't fear him but her own emotions. He'd watched the fire in her eyes when desire consumed her and then when shame overcame her at her reaction to his kiss. His prim and proper governess was only a front for the passionate woman Sara kept hidden. And he eagerly waited to unwrap the layers and watch her blossom when she accepted the passion and love between them.

"You appear pleased with yourself this morning for a groom whose bride slept in a different bedchamber." Lord Whetham cackled.

Referring to Sara as his bride only widened Somerville's grin. "Aye."

He settled in his chair and waited while the footman poured his tea and another placed a plate in front of him. Somerville shook the napkin out across his lap and began to eat. He would've explained more to his in-laws if it weren't for the servants standing nearby, waiting to serve them at a moment's notice. While the gossip of them sleeping in separate beds last night had already spread amongst the servants, he refused to supply them with any further prattle to add to the false rumors already circulating about Sara.

Lady Whetham signaled to the butler to clear the room. Once the door closed behind the servants, she confronted Somerville. "Why did Sara sleep in Mairi's bedchamber?"

Somerville spread jam across his bread and took a bite before responding. "I assume Sara became confused about where to sleep when she noticed the removal of her belongings from her bedchamber."

Lord Whetham flipped a page of the newspaper. "Most brides sleep with their grooms the evening of their wedding."

"Stuart," Lady Whetham reprimanded.

"I am only stating the obvious, my dear. Either the boy is out of practice or he finds fault with this bride." Whetham lowered the paper. "Which is it?"

Somerville chuckled. "None of your affair and far from the truth. I only chose not to force myself upon my wife. She suffered enough with the stress of our wedding yesterday, and I did not want to overwhelm her."

"While that was a kind gesture, I fear it only gave the servants room to gossip that your union is not genuine," Lady Whetham stated.

Somerville cocked his eyebrow. "I dare any of them to speak unwell about my wife."

Lady Whetham reached across to pat Somerville's hand. "I do not believe they will out of spite. However, you are well aware how someone can misconstrue an innocent comment they may overhear."

Somerville nodded that he understood how Sara, sleeping in Mairi's bedchamber, sent a message that their marriage might be a sham. He'd married Sara to prevent any more false rumors from spreading and to protect her virtue. He needed to speak with Sara and explain the delicacy of their situation and how they must share a suite while residing with his in-laws. After they return to Scotland, if she chose not to give their marriage a chance, then they could have separate bedchambers. However, while they stayed in London, they must present a united front of affection in front of others.

"I will speak with Sara this morning."

Lady Whetham smiled. "Excellent."

Lord Whetham harrumphed. "Hopefully, you do more than speak with her."

Lady Whetham swatted at her husband. "Incorrigible as ever."

Somerville laughed at how his in-laws teased each other. He had shared a similar marriage with Claudia. He had known Claudia since they were children. Theirs was a marriage arranged before birth. Their families had visited one another often, and as a result, they'd grown to be best friends before they married. They were each other's first, from their first kiss to their marital bed. Their love was a companionable deep affection they would've shared forever. When Claudia died, he'd suffered a loss so profound he believed he would never find love again. Nor had he wanted to. Claudia's love had been enough for him. He'd lost not only his wife but his best friend too.

However, ever since Sara entered his life, he had awakened from his misery to see the brightness of a new beginning for him and Mairi. Sara brought new emotions to the surface, making him eager to see what their future might hold for them. Last night's kiss showed him the passion simmering between them wasn't one-sided. He couldn't wait to explore the desire he felt for her. Now, only to woo her into seeing how worthy she was for him. He wouldn't allow the differences in their stations separate them. By the time they returned to Scotland, he would prove to Sara that their bond was unbreakable. And no threat or rumors would keep them apart.

Somerville patted his lips with the napkin. "If you will excuse me, I need to speak with my wife."

Lady Whetham waved to him to stay seated. "Allow me. I want to invite her to take tea with me this afternoon at Lady Radwell's and then visit the shops."

Somerville frowned. "Perhaps outings are too soon."

Lady Whetham smiled with patience. "Trust me. I would never place Sara in an uncomfortable situation. I will protect her as if she were my daughter."

"Very well. But only if she wants to," Somerville conceded.

Somerville leaned back as Lady Whetham strolled out of the breakfast room. He didn't want Sara to feel pressured to venture into society yet if it made her uncomfortable. Also, he worried whoever threatened her would confront her if he weren't there to protect her.

"I think I will join them on their outing," Somerville murmured.

Lord Whetham folded the paper next to his plate. "You cannot follow the girl every second of her life. It will only draw forth another set of rumors about how you do not trust her."

"I care less about anyone's opinion. I only care about Sara's safety."

"Then trust Marian to see after Sara's welfare."

Somerville blew out a frustrated breath. He understood his in-laws' intention, but couldn't they see how delicate of a flower Sara was? She hadn't been born into their society and didn't understand how to navigate her way through difficult situations. The vultures would be out and waiting to catch her alone. He wondered if he should send word for Lady Courtland to accompany them. Then he remembered the Courtlands would be preparing for their return to Scotland.

He sighed with defeat. "I will trust her in this one excursion. But if anyone dares to insult my wife today, they will feel my wrath."

Lord Whetham shook the newspaper out again. "Then let us pray for a quiet outing."

Somerville didn't believe any prayer would keep Sara from getting hurt today. His mother-in-law held the best of intentions, but he had seen first-hand the cruelty of the ton. They were a vindictive lot who set out to destroy anyone in their path. However, they would discover Sara wouldn't be their latest victim. Not with the consequences he would deal if anyone dared to step out of line.

His wrath would destroy all.

Chapter Four

False Rumors

SARA AWAKENED TO A gentle pat against her cheek. Her eyelids fluttered open to Mairi standing over her, clutching her favorite doll. Her gaze drifted around the room as her disorientation faded away. She had stolen into the child's bedchamber after she discovered the servants had moved her belongings without her consent. Her only conclusion was that they were now in Somerville's suite.

Ian.

The very person and room she wished to avoid. Her face grew warm as the memories of the kiss they'd shared rushed forward. She still couldn't believe how wantonly she had behaved. What must the duke think of her? He surely held regrets once he remembered his behavior in his inebriated state.

She slid upward onto the cot and held out her arms. "Good morning, poppet."

Mairi jumped into her arms. "Good morning, Momma. Why are you sleeping in my room? Should you not be with Poppa?"

The innocence of the child's question caught her off guard. While Sara wanted nothing more than to have awakened in Somerville's arms, she was also realistic. Her fantasies would never come true. Too many obstacles stood between them.

Sara brushed the hair from Mairi's face. "Do you remember how frightened you were on our first night here? And I slept with you to show how safe you were."

Mairi nodded.

"Yesterday frightened me with how my life had changed after I married your father and I wanted to sleep with my favorite person to feel safe," Sara explained.

"Poppa will keep you safe too."

Sara smiled at Mairi's unwavering devotion to her father's abilities. The duke had more than proven his determination to protect her from the evilness haunting her every step. It was the other emotions he stirred to life that frightened her. She feared he might break her heart because he didn't share the same affection for her as she did him. While she felt honored by his protection, she wished it wasn't the reason for their marriage. Those thoughts led to her disappointment with herself. She must tamp down her ungratefulness or she would find herself living a miserable existence.

Sara wrapped Mairi in her arms for a hug. "Yes, I believe he will. Now, shall we dress for the day and enjoy breakfast together?"

Mairi hopped off the bed and ran to dress in the outfit Sara had laid out for her. "Hurry, Momma, I heard Poppa go downstairs a little while ago."

Sara rose off the cot and helped Mairi to dress. She brushed her hair into place and added a ribbon. "Go below and I will join you after I change."

Sara smiled with fondness as Mairi tore along the hallway like a hellion. She had come so far since she had first met the girl. Once forlorn, she now behaved with the energy of a boisterous child. She must speak with Somerville about Mairi's care since they were now wed. Sara wanted to continue her duties but understood she must also fulfill the responsibilities of a duchess. However, she wanted Somerville to understand she wished to involve herself in Mairi's upbringing as much as he would allow.

She left Mairi's bedchamber and walked along the hallway to Somerville's suite, where she paused outside the door, unsure of entering without his permission. Granted, she held every right to enter, but it still felt awkward. It was his personal space, and when she entered, the intimacy of their situation would assault her senses with every desire she kept hidden. However, she held no other option since her belongings were mingled with his. She had neglected not noticing her things. Somerville had dominated her attention with his overwhelming presence that left her more enamored of him than ever.

"No need to hesitate, my dear. 'Tis your bedchamber too. If it is Somerville you wish to avoid, no need. He is belowstairs eating breakfast with Lord Whetham and Mairi."

Sara swung around with her hand clutched near her bosom, so lost in her thoughts that Lady Whetham had startled her with her appearance. The countess smiled at Sara with kindness and appeared to understand Sara's awkwardness. Before she could respond, Lady Whetham ushered Sara inside and closed the door behind them. She didn't hesitate to cross to the wardrobe holding Sara's clothing. Sara watched the countess with trepidation about what she had planned for her. She didn't dare contradict or refuse the lady. Especially since the lady had only ever put her at ease and accepted her into Somerville and Mairi's life without question.

"I believe this will look lovely on you for today's outing." Lady Whetham held out Sara's best dress.

It was a modest dress she wore when her friends invited her to their gatherings. A plain day dress that offered her the ability to blend in without drawing attention to herself. She'd never held enough coin to afford anything elaborate, nor was it her taste to.

"Outing?" Sara squeaked, now aware of Lady Whetham's intention.

Lady Whetham bustled around the room, gathering clothing for Sara. "I would like you to join me today for tea at Lady Radwell's. Then I thought we would visit some shoppes in Mayfair to purchase the items for your wardrobe as a duchess. We will stop at my modiste for your measurements and to choose patterns for new dresses."

Sara stared at the floor in shame at how she disgraced the duke with her meager belongings. She must agree to Lady Whetham's wishes so as not to embarrass Somerville or his family any more than she already had. She was out of her element on how to respond to the countess's thoughtful offer. So she stayed quiet, hoping her silence would go unnoticed. However, Lady Whetham was too keen not to notice.

She guided Sara to the settee and sat next to her. Marian needed to tread with careful regard so as not to upset the young lady. However, Sara had much to learn since she was now Somerville's wife. Marian only wanted to help guide Sara into society with no fanfare or drama. She only suggested today's outing to introduce her to the friendlier side of the aristocracy. From what Somerville had shared of Sara's friendships in Scotland, Marian wished to introduce Sara to other ladies with the same endearing characteristics.

Marian placed her hand over Sara's clutched fists in her lap. "We will not leave today if that is your wish. I only suggested the outing to help ease you into society."

Sara raised her head at the sincerity in Lady Whetham's voice. "I do not wish to disgrace you or the duke. I fear I will only embarrass you among your friends, and I have no clue what I need to purchase. Nor do I wish to spend the duke's money in a foolish fashion."

"Oh, dear, you will never bring shame to our family. We could not be prouder to call you one of our own. My only thought is to introduce you to like-minded ladies who share the same qualities as your friends. It never hurts to surround yourself with enough friends who would defend your honor if necessary. As for spending Ian's money, it is your right, my dear, as his wife." Marian chuckled. "I do not insist on visiting the shoppes because I find fault with you, only because I wish to offer you any guidance you may need."

Sara ran a hand along her wrinkled skirts. "Your offer is very kind, Lady Whetham."

"I think we can dispose of Lady Whetham now that you are family. I insist you call me Marian."

Sara raised her wide gaze to Lady Whetham. "I could not dare."

Marian's eyes twinkled. "Why ever not?"

"'Tis most inappropriate, not to mention disrespectful."

Marian waved her hand in the air. "Nonsense."

Sara dug her teeth into her bottom lip, unsure if she should ask her next question. However, if she were to be a member of this family, then she needed to understand the reason for Lord and Lady Whetham's acceptance of her as Somerville's wife and Mairi's new mother. "May I ask the reason you welcome me with warmth into your family?"

Marian sighed as she noticed the insecurity Sara suffered. From what she had learned, Sara had lived a simple life raised by her grandmother. She'd learned how to survive on her own after her grandmother passed away. The drama the girl had to endure would've changed anyone. However, Sara had kept her gentleness and innocence in the face of her adversity. Most families would've felt threatened by someone of Sara's background infiltrating their family. However, Sara had no ulterior motives. Marian knew her daughter would've found comfort in Sara's appearance in Ian's and Mairi's lives. That was reason enough for her and Stuart to accept Sara so warmly into their fold.

"Has Ian ever spoken to you about his marriage to our daughter?"

Sara shook her head.

Marian smiled wistfully. "I will not share the intimate details about the union. It is only fair for Somerville to tell you when he is ready. We arranged the marriage with Ian's parents before Ian and Claudia were born. We threw them together at every opportunity throughout their lives to prepare them for the fate we arranged for them. They married each other as the best of friends and were compatible in every aspect imaginable. While their love was unique in its own way, it lacked the passion they might have found if we allowed them to find their soulmates on their own."

Sara blushed at Lady Whetham's bold declaration and twisted her hands with nervous thoughts. Did the lady suspect Sara's wanton feelings for the duke? Perhaps she should've kept her curiosity to herself.

"Somerville never mentioned the depth of his love for your daughter. But when I arrived, I realized he must have loved her deeply for how her death still affects him."

"Yes, Claudia's death left Ian with a grief we feared he would never recover from. However, ever since you entered his life, you have brought him out of his despair and given him a second chance at love. Because of the happiness you have brought to Ian and Mairi, we cannot do anything but accept you into our family. Our daughter would have insisted for us to love you the way Ian and Mairi do."

"He does not ... I ... We are not ..." Sara stuttered.

Lady Whetham winked at Sara. "Not yet, anyway."

Sara sat stunned by the reason the Whethams held no qualms about Somerville marrying her. Would they accept her if they knew how she had dreamed of being Somerville's wife and Mairi's mother? She stared into Lady Whetham's eyes and realized the lady already understood the depth of Sara's feelings for Somerville and she couldn't be more thrilled. Her acceptance overwhelmed Sara enough for her to reach across and hug Lady Whetham. She pulled back in shock at her affection. However, the lady pulled her back and gave her the comforting hug Sara needed more than she thought.

Lady Whetham pulled away and rose, wiping her eyes. "Now, shall I send in your maid to help you dress? Or would you prefer to stay at home?"

Sara rose and followed Lady Whetham. "No need to send in the maid. If you give me a few minutes, I will make myself presentable to join you. Thank you for the invitation."

Lady Whetham nodded. "Very well. Take your time and join us in the breakfast room when you are ready."

After the countess left, Sara wandered toward the bed where Lady Whetham had laid out her attire. Her gaze drifted across the length of the bed where Somerville had slept. A place she should've slept too had she not allowed her doubts to keep her away. Was Lady Whetham correct about Somerville's feelings for her? Did she have the courage to discover for herself? Or would her insecurities keep her from finding love?

Sara rushed to prepare herself for the outing with the countess. She didn't dare dwell on her thoughts for too long. They would only lead to more questions she was too much of a coward to understand. She would face the dilemma of where to sleep later. Sara understood the need to present to the staff and society that their marriage wasn't a farce.

Now only to convince her heart.

False Rumors

Sara hovered in the doorway, not wanting to interrupt the familiar intimacy of Somerville, Mairi, and the Whethams. The interaction between them was one Sara had always imagined for herself. The banter and affection they gave Mairi warmed her heart. She smiled at how Somerville held Mairi on his lap as she ate away at a scone smeared with jam. He never once scowled at Mairi's sticky mess coming into contact with his clothing. He laughed as he wiped away at a spot that fell on his shirt sleeve. Instead of intruding, she stood back, watching them as an interloper. When she actually wanted to sit next to Somerville and share in the amusement of Mairi.

She stepped back to allow them their moment as a family when Lord Whetham took notice of her in the doorway. "There she is and looks as lovely as ever."

Sara blushed and lowered her head. "You are too kind, Lord Whetham."

He rose and offered his arm to escort her to the seat next to Somerville at the table. "Stuart, my dear. There is no need for formalities since we are now family."

"Exactly what I told her," Lady Whetham replied.

Sara settled in her seat and offered a shy smile to everyone while the servants poured her tea and set a plate before her. They soon resumed their conversation, leaving her to eat and watch them. While Somerville conversed with his in-laws and answered Mairi's curious questions, his unwavering gaze stayed focused on her. Warmth settled over Sara, wrapping her in Ian's adoration.

Each time she met his glance, he gave her a smile that made her blush turn brighter. The smile held a mixture of patience and kindness, with an underlying component of desire. For him to stare at her so blatantly in front of his child and in-laws was a scandal itself. His actions were out of character. That only led Sara to believe either the effects of his overindulgence yesterday still affected him or it was an act to convince the servants and Lord and Lady Whetham their marriage was real. In her confusion, she had no clue how to respond other than to avert her gaze.

Somerville wanted to chuckle at Sara's reaction to his interest. Except he had no desire to draw attention to her. The blush gracing her cheeks only pushed his desire to the next level and made him wonder if it covered her entire body. Having scandalous thoughts in the company of his family was most inappropriate and unlike him. Sara brought out a side of him he wanted to explore with her. However, his wife wouldn't find the same amusement in the situation as he did. Wife. Calling Sara his wife held a much more befitting ring than calling her his governess.

"Poppa, when will it snow?" Mairi asked.

Everyone laughed at her question, though none of them had the answer. Mairi had been asking the same question since they arrived, and much to her disappointment, it still hadn't occurred.

"Maybe if we close our eyes, cross our fingers, and make a wish, it will happen soon." Sara wiped a smidge of jam off Mairi's cheek.

"Can we?" Mairi asked, bouncing on Somerville's lap.

Sara reached out for Mairi's hand. "Now close your eyes." She helped Mairi cross her fingers. "Our fingers are crossed. So now we make our wish."

Sara should've wished for the snow to help Mairi's chances, but her heart wished for the impossible instead. She heard Mairi's whispered wish for snow when she peeked an eye open to see Somerville's eyes closed and his lips moving in a wish of his own. Once he finished, he opened his eyes and directed his gaze at her again. However, Sara couldn't mistake the smoldering glance for more than what it was. Pure desire. The duke's behavior was more wicked than she imagined.

"Did you make a wish, Poppa?"

Somerville smiled at his daughter. "Yes, poppet. Though I am sorry to disappoint you, but it was not for snow."

"That is all right." Mairi patted his cheek with her sticky fingers. "I hope it comes true for you."

"So do I," Somerville murmured with a wink at Sara.

Sara glanced away and met Lady Whetham's amused expression, which only flustered her more. She didn't dare look in Lord Whetham's direction when she heard his amused laughter. He would probably wink at her too. An occurrence that happened too much for her comfort today. Instead, she added more sugar than necessary to her tea. Anything to distract her from what she assumed related to her.

Lady Whetham rose and walked to Somerville, lifting Mairi off his lap. "Shall we get you clean for the day, young lady?"

"An excellent idea, Lady Whetham. Then perhaps my granddaughter could read me a story."

"Silly Grandfather. I cannot read complete books yet."

"Then you can help me with the more difficult words."

The Whethams left with Mairi walking between them, holding their hands. Just like Somerville, they never minded their granddaughter's sticky hands. Their only thought was to spend as much time with her during their visit. The family was a rarity among the aristocracy. While most never allowed their young children to dine with them, they did so at every chance. The

Whethams and Sara's friends showed her a different way of life. It was a refreshing change from the other households she had governed in.

"Did you sleep well?" Somerville murmured, breaking through Sara's thoughts.

She smoothed the napkin across her lap to keep herself occupied instead of staring deeply into Somerville's gaze. "Yes."

Somerville reached across and slipped his palm over her hand. "Do not feel pressured to accompany Marian today. Your entrance into society can wait."

"I wish to join her today," Sara whispered.

"Sara."

Sara raised her gaze. "Yes, Your Grace?"

"Ian," Somerville insisted. "Say the word and we shall return to Scotland. I do not care for the niceties my mother-in-law insists upon."

Sara ignored his preference for her to call him by his Christian name. "Lady Whetham's offer is out of kindness, and she promised none of her plans will overwhelm me. I want to belong in your world with no embarrassment on my part. And in doing so, I must meet your peers and dress accordingly."

Somerville squeezed Sara's hand. "There has never been, nor will there ever be, a moment where you will embarrass me."

The heat searing from his touch warmed the sincerity of his words. His faith in her was the very reason she must join Lady Whetham today. To prove to his family and friends that she was worthy of his praise. She promised to give the new opportunities in her path a chance. To accept her place in the unfamiliar domain that was now her future. Somerville made every attempt to accept her as she was. Now she must return the gesture. She didn't have to change who she was. She only needed to open herself to fresh possibilities that would enrich her life and those she loved. To do so, she must believe Somerville was sincere in his behavior toward her.

"What are your plans for the day?" Sara hoped Somerville would allow her to change the course of their conversation.

Somerville leaned back in his chair but kept his hand covering hers. He was reluctant to stop touching Sara. Her not pulling away gave him hope that she enjoyed the intimacy as much as he did.

"After some paperwork, I thought I would take Mairi to the park. Perhaps spoil her with a visit to the chocolate shoppe."

Sara smiled. "She would adore time alone with you."

"Mmm," Somerville murmured. He neglected to inform Sara of his entire plan.

Sara withdrew her hands from his and laid her napkin on the table. "I should gather my bonnet and wrap."

Somerville rose and pulled Sara's chair back to help her rise. "I hope you have a pleasant day." Before stepping away, he placed a gentle kiss against her cheek.

Sara gripped the back of the chair to keep herself from melting into a muddled mess. She could only describe Ian's smile as a lethal weapon to destroy the walls surrounding her heart. She wanted to sway into his arms from the kiss alone. Any reason for him to kiss her as passionately as he had the evening before, a scene that would shock anyone if they were to come upon them.

Instead, she rushed out of the room to put distance between them before she foolhardily embarrassed both of them with her actions. She thought she heard his soft chuckle following her but didn't dare turn around to find out. Ever since they spoke their wedding vows, Somerville had become a changed gentleman, one who left her unsure how to react and flustered beyond belief.

Or Ian, she should say.

Somerville chuckled as Sara hurried away. His behavior confused her, but no more than it confused him. He prided himself on his impeccable decorum, but with Sara, she stirred something to life in him that varied between a lighthearted scoundrel and a wicked rake whose only purpose was to seduce her into his bed. He enjoyed teasing her until her cheeks bloomed like a red rose and desire flared in her eyes. It was then that he realized he wasn't the only one who held curiosity about where their marriage might lead.

"Should I be worried about your intentions for the dear girl?" Lady Whetham interrupted his musings.

Somerville smirked. "I have no idea what you refer to."

Lady Whetham shook her head with a hint of a smile. "You are forgetting, my dear boy, how I have known you your entire life. Do not charm me with your innocence."

"I am wounded by your accusation."

Lady Whetham rolled her eyes. "What is the term you Scottish utter? Bollocks."

Somerville gasped in amusement. "Why, Lady Whetham, how improper of you. Perhaps my wife's past profession as a governess will rub off on you while she keeps you company today. It is obvious you need her influence more than she needs yours."

Lady Whetham swatted his arm with her reticule. "You are still an impish lad who is as incorrigible as ever."

Somerville bowed toward Lady Whetham. "I only have the best of intentions for Sara."

"See that you do." She paused in the doorway. "I am pleased to see you returning to your old self. We have missed you."

His mother-in-law strolled away without waiting for his response. He had withdrawn after Claudia's death and, as a result, hadn't been there for his in-laws, leaving them to suffer alone with their grief. He suffered from guilt since they were like parents to him. After his parents died, they had stepped in and offered him the same guidance, love, and support his own would have. However, he had neglected them when they needed him the most. He hoped their visit would heal the sorrow between them.

As for his intentions for Sara, he hoped to make her his bride in every sense.

Chapter Five

False Rumors

Sara stopped at the display of ribbons as she waited for Marian to finish with the details of Sara's new wardrobe. She trusted the lady with her decisions on what was best. Soon, Sara must make those decisions herself once she became accustomed to the lifestyle her title expected. For now, she would accept Marian and her friends' guidance.

Marian had worn her down throughout the day not to address her as Lady Whetham. From each kind word she expressed to her friends and the simple gestures of affection, Sara had grown more comfortable around the lady. Marian made Sara feel like she was one of her own. The ladies she introduced Sara to had been more than welcoming and accepted Sara without judgment. She allowed herself to relax around them, the danger behind her marriage to Somerville forgotten.

She had yet to bring herself to address him as Ian, even in her thoughts. Because if she so much as allowed herself to, her thoughts turned most wicked. However, the brush of his lips across her cheek this morning and the intimate way he'd held her hand under the table consumed her thoughts, often distracting her from the surrounding conversations. However, luck prevailed during those moments when the conversation didn't focus on her but on other topics.

She sifted through the ribbons and marveled at their delicacy. As with the other garments presented to her while shopping, Sara marveled at the difference in clothing for a commoner versus a member of society. Soon the fabrics would adorn her body and alter her appearance. However, they wouldn't change her attitude about how she presented herself. Except they would give her the confidence she lacked.

She wished her grandmother were alive to offer her wisdom on the changes occurring in Sara's life. Her words would help ground her as they always did. Sara had never had a mother and father to guide her through life, but her grandmother had more than offered her the love and affection she'd needed to thrive. Because of her grandmother's influence, she'd become the lady she was today. After spending the day with Lady Whetham, Sara realized the words *mother* and *father* were only titles. It was the attention a person paid you that held an impact on how special they were to you.

The bell over the door rang as another customer walked inside. Sara raised her head to see Mairi skipping toward her and Somerville following behind with a smile. Sara brightened at their appearance. A perfect ending to her outing with Marian.

Sara bent down. "Did you enjoy your visit to the park?"

"We want you to come too, Momma."

"Is that so?" Sara peeked at Somerville and noticed a sparkle of mischief twinkling in his gaze. "Well then, shall we ask if your grandmother would like to join us too?"

"I will ask her." Mairi skipped across the shoppe toward Marian.

Somerville gripped her elbow to help her rise. "She insisted we find you to join us."

Sara thought Somerville would release her once she rose. However, he kept his possessive hold by pulling her closer. She pressed her hand against his coat to steady herself. "And I suppose you had no objection to her demands," Sara teased. She could be mischievous too.

"Not in the slightest, my dear. In truth, I must confess I might have encouraged her demand with a suggestion or two," Somerville confessed.

She smoothed her hand across the luxurious fabric. "Has anyone ever told you how incorrigible you are, Your Grace?"

Somerville threw back his head, laughing. He found immense pleasure in their teasing. "Why, just this morning, Marian might have mentioned it."

"I dare not ask what prompted that conversation."

Somerville pulled Sara deeper into his embrace. "I would be more than pleased to share with you the reason."

The rest of the world faded away as Somerville held her. She lost herself in the teasing glint in his eyes that reflected his enjoyment of her company. Gossip would spread about their intimacy in such a public setting. However, Sara had not a care for other people's opinions. Especially since Somerville behaved as if their embrace was the most natural act in the world. She should care, but she'd learned long ago that people would gossip to amuse themselves no matter the innocence of a situation.

When someone cleared their throat behind them, Sara jumped and stepped away from Somerville. The spell between them broke at the interruption. She turned to see Marian and Mairi watching them. Marian smiled as if she had conspired with Mairi to appear at the dress shoppe. Which was ridiculous. Wasn't it? She glanced between Marian and Somerville, then landed her gaze on Mairi. Each of them held a look of innocence, proving Sara must've imagined it all. It was only a coincidence they'd ended their shopping with a park nearby.

"Mairi has informed me they have arrived for a walk in the park. However, I must decline. I have another visit to make," Marian pleaded her excuse.

"Thank you for inviting me today. I have enjoyed myself, Marian."

Marian smiled. "As have I, my dear. Enjoy your walk and I will see everyone at home for dinner."

They left the shoppe and walked to the park. Once they entered through the gates, Mairi skipped ahead of them, leaving Somerville and Sara alone.

He drew her arm through the crook of his elbow. To anyone watching, they would assume he was a husband smitten with his wife, enjoying the time spent with their child. Not a duke who had just married his governess yesterday to protect her from an unknown villain who had yet to mock their sudden marriage. However, the threat loomed nearby. Sara shivered at the very thought.

Somerville stopped them, unwrapped his scarf from around his neck, and draped it around Sara. "You are cold. We should return to the carriage."

"I am fine, Your Grace."

Somerville frowned. "How is it that my mother-in-law won the battle to be called Marian but I am still Your Grace?"

Sara cringed at the hurt in Somerville's voice that she'd honored Marian's request, but she still hadn't honored his wish. She had wronged him. "Ian."

He tugged on the scarf, bringing her flush against him. "Do you have any idea how I hunger to ravish your lips at this exact moment?"

Sara gasped, glancing around to see who was watching them. "You would not dare."

Somerville cocked his eyebrow. "Would I not?"

The mischievous glint in Somerville's eyes should've been warning enough for Sara not to push him, but uttering his title would be her downfall. "Somerville," Sara warned.

"I warned you." Somerville dipped his head to ravish Sara with a kiss that left her speechless.

He stole her breath away with the demand of his lips upon hers. They were the force of a man hungered for the taste of her. Sara had thought their embrace from the evening before was a testament to the desire between them, but it paled compared to the kisses he ravished from her lips. One kiss ended, only for another to begin. Each one more demanding than the last. His tongue stroked his needs against hers with the force of the passion he unleashed on her.

Sara clutched at the lapels of his coat to find an anchor before she floated away from the sheer pleasure of Ian kissing her. Her inexperience left her clueless about how to respond, but she allowed her body's reaction to guide her to return Ian's affection with her heart's desire. Her tongue danced against his with her need to savor Ian's unique blend of masculinity.

His response to Sara saying his name would leave the gossipmongers tittering from his shameless display of affection for his former governess. But when Sara whispered, "Ian," he lost all common sense. His erratic behavior left him shocked that he couldn't care less who might witness his behavior or what they might say. Ever the prim and proper duke. His peers would now view him as a gentleman who didn't have a concern if he caused a scandal.

But he couldn't stop from losing himself in her sweetness. He captured each of her sighs in his soul. They helped to heal his heartache and flourish into a love he had never experienced before. He should pull away, but his heart begged him to prolong the kiss for an eternity.

He traced his tongue across her lips before plunging back into her mouth to draw out her moan of desire. His soul had a more powerful reaction to her moan than her soft sighs. He longed to hear her scream his name with the pleasure he wanted to show her.

However, the universe had other plans for him. Or more like his daughter. Mairi tugged on his coat, calling his name and pulling him back to the brink of sanity.

"Poppa! Momma! Look, my wish came true."

"Ian." Sara sighed.

Somerville pulled away with reluctance and looked to the sky to watch the smallest of snowflakes drifting down upon them. It would seem it was the day for wishes to come true. His gaze returned to Sara to see her press her fingers against her lips and stare at him with a sense of wonder. Her sigh of his name when he pulled away from their kiss granted him hope that his wish had come true. Soon, he would break through Sara's defenses to capture her heart as his own. For now, he would continue to show her how special she was to him.

He lifted Mairi in his arms and twirled her around, laughing with her when her giggles grew louder. "A miracle indeed."

Sara lowered her fingers from her lips and clutched them in front of her to keep from joining their embrace. While Ian's kiss spoke of his need to claim her, it wasn't an open invitation to instigate herself into a special moment between father and daughter. However, Ian held a different opinion and swung an arm around her waist, twirling her around with them. Sara couldn't help but join in their laughter.

"Poppa, stop! You are making me dizzy." Mairi giggled.

Ian stopped and set Mairi on her feet. Sara tipped her head back to admire the snowflakes falling heavier upon them. Perhaps it was a day for miracles. It all seemed so impossible to believe. However, with each minute that passed, Sara believed all her wishes would come true. Ian's kiss gave her the confidence to recognize the impossible was within her grasp.

She only had to keep believing.

False Rumors

Somerville leaned back in the chair behind the desk. Since their return from the park, he'd found it impossible to focus. The kiss he'd shared with Sara dominated his thoughts. Hell, it wasn't a kiss they shared, when he'd staked his claim and ravished her for all of London to take notice. It was more than obvious that he'd lost his sensible side with how he neglected his daughter, because sampling Sara's sweetness seemed more pertinent. At least his daughter held the good sense not to wander too far away. He must focus on his duties, but thoughts of Sara snared his attention, an act she didn't even realize she held the power of. It only made her more enticing.

He raked his hand through his hair. He needed to get his emotions under control before he frightened her with the overwhelming desire he felt for her. Somerville never imagined this type of passion existed. He'd watched his fellow peers fall victim to the lust flittering around their society but never believed he would experience the intense desire.

With Claudia, they'd shared a comfortable passion that kept him satisfied. Their companionable love had more than sufficed for their lack of desire for one another. However, with Sara, he craved more than simple lovemaking. He hungered for their souls to merge as one and to explore the passion simmering between them. And from how she returned his kisses, it was without a doubt that Sara wished the same.

With a sigh, he sat forward to sift through the mail that had arrived during his absence. He tossed the invitations to the side. He would sit with Sara to go through them and decide on which events she wished to attend. If she wasn't ready to venture into the social scene, he would support her decision. If he wasn't guilt-ridden about extending their visit with the Whethams, he would rush them back to Scotland so she could enter society with her friends by her side instead. However, for now, they would maneuver their way amongst the London ton the best they could.

Distracted with thoughts of Sara dressed in an elegant ballgown while he led her on a waltz across the ballroom floor, he failed to notice the familiar script on the envelope he opened. It wasn't until he glanced down at the paper that he realized the villain who had terrorized Sara and her friends the past year had struck again. He had been waiting for the threatening letter to arrive since he spoke his vows with Sara yesterday.

Your Grace, the Duke of Somerville,

With someone of your high esteem, I should offer you my congratulations on your joyous union with the lovely Miss Abbott. However, I find nothing but dissatisfaction with the marriage vows you spoke to your governess. You have partaken in the hierarchy's fall that has withstood years of exclusivity because of a tenderness you believe you feel for someone of the lower class. Do you imagine the title Sara now holds will erase her past?

I fear it will only draw more attention to the poor girl. Especially once everyone learns of her origins. A tragic tale that will only secure you and your new bride to be outcasts among those who used to admire your status in society. Have you told your wife about what you have learned about her parents?

Obviously not by the indecent scene you caused in the park today. And with your daughter present too, no less. For shame, Your Grace. You allowed your cock to rule your actions. Now, when I reveal the truth about your wife's parents, everyone will shun the duchess and force your return to Scotland. You should have never brought Sara to London. Because of her, your family will live in disgrace. Young Mairi never stood a chance once Miss Sara Abbott entered your lives.

However, by the time I finish with you, you will not even be welcome in your beloved Scotland. Know this, Somerville, 'tis your fault my vengeance has grown to a higher level. If you had not meddled in Sara's past, then I might've been persuaded to end this injustice. But you delved into issues that were none of your concern. You've left me with no other option than to strike until I have ruined you, as you are set to ruin me.

This leaves me to speculate that your sweet governess, now wife, has no clue what you have discovered about her past. Some secrets are meant to be kept hidden. So I can only ask, why are you keeping secrets? Are you ashamed of Sara?

Not a promising start to your marriage.

We shall speak soon.

Somerville gritted his teeth as he crumpled the parchment in his fist. The bastard had struck again, but only with innuendoes, nothing threatening toward Sara. He wanted to leave for Scotland, but trouble would only follow them. He must draw the villain into his trap for them to live in peace. To do so, he would require the Courtlands' help, along with their other friends from Scotland. The more people showing their support for their union would dissuade any rumors that might strike. Also, Sara needed her friends to surround her more than ever.

He unwrinkled the paper and slid it inside his suit coat. He needed to share it with Courtland. They would devise a plan to draw out the culprits who set out to destroy four ladies whose only crime was falling in love. Somerville couldn't wait to destroy the evilness that had overtaken their lives the past few months. Falling in love with Sara was the only shining light from the ordeal.

He strode out of the study and requested his carriage. As he waited in the foyer for his coat, Sara's and Mairi's laughter drifted from the library. He longed to join them, but arranging for Sara's friends to join them in London required his attention. He must inform Courtland of the threat so he could assist Somerville with the necessary arrangements. Only once Sara's friends arrived could he admit the secrets he had withheld from her when he convinced her to marry him. He only hoped she forgave him and saw he'd done so to keep her protected.

Love could not prosper with secrets.

Chapter Six

False Rumors

SARA STOOD INSIDE MAIRI's bedchamber, watching Ian's nightly bedtime ritual with his daughter. The Whethams had left to attend the opera with their friends, which left Sara and Ian alone for the evening. He'd ignored Sara during the evening meal and appeared preoccupied with troubled thoughts, so it surprised her when he asked her to join him. She thought he would prefer to partake in his usual evening pursuits and not concern himself with entertaining his wife.

However, Ian's mood had shifted while tucking Mairi into bed. Her usual excuses not to fall asleep amused him, as they always did, and brought forth a smile she hadn't seen throughout the meal. She didn't understand what bothered him but hoped it wasn't because of her. Perhaps she should apologize for her scandalous behavior in the park to ease his troubles.

"Now, young lady, no more stalling. You must fall asleep for another grand adventure tomorrow." Ian kissed Mairi's forehead.

"More snow?" Mairi asked.

Ian chuckled. "That might require more wishes. Since you can only make one wish a day, you must close your eyes for sleep now."

Mairi's face scrunched together as she squeezed her eyes tight. "Good night, Poppa and Momma."

Sara stepped toward the bed and bent over to kiss Mairi's cheek. "Sweet dreams, darling girl."

Ian blew out the candle. However, he kept the door ajar for the hallway light to stream through. He wrapped his arm around Sara's waist before she could put distance between them. She didn't want him to feel as if he had to entertain her for the evening if he had other plans. But she stayed silent as he guided them to their bedchamber.

"I hope you do not mind, but I requested tea and dessert to be brought to our suite. I thought we could talk until bedtime. Unless you wish to read."

A tea set and plates of cake sat on the table in front of the settee. He might not have requested a romantic atmosphere, but the servants had decided otherwise with the flowers and candles spread throughout the suite. His thoughtfulness kept surprising Sara with each of his acts of kindness. He understood the difficulty she struggled with to fit into his world and only wanted to ease her discomfort.

She squeezed his arm. "I would enjoy spending a quiet evening in our suite. Unless you have other plans you must attend to. I would understand if you need to leave."

Ian tucked a stray curl behind Sara's ear. "My only wish is to relax with my wife this evening."

Sara offered him a timid smile as she pulled away from him to sit on the settee. She poured the tea and waited for him to join her. When she raised her gaze, she gulped as Ian tugged at his cravat until it came apart. He laid it atop his suit coat he had taken off. The top buttons of his shirt were undone and his vest discarded too. Sara had never seen a gentleman in this state of undress. Perhaps she had misinterpreted his evening of relaxation.

"Ah ... that is ... um ..." Sara couldn't utter a coherent string of words to question the situation.

All she was aware of was how the butterflies in her stomach had taken flight again, and a warmth overcame her at her reaction to her husband's intimate act of undressing in front of her. While he still wore most of his clothing, he aroused her imagination about how he might look if he were to finish undressing.

Sara held no clue how adorable she was, biting her bottom lip as she stared at him. Ian had never thought discarding the annoying articles of clothing he must wear outside his bedchamber would fluster his wife to the degree it had. He should continue his act of a proper gentleman who would never dare shock his wife with inappropriate behavior, but after their kiss today, he wanted to share with her the most intimate of acts. Even if it were only to lounge in their bedchamber without the stuffiness of a cravat, vest, and suit coat.

If he suggested for her to undo the top buttons on her dress, Sara would flee their bedchamber again. And tonight, he wanted her as close as she would allow. Not only because of the threat he'd received today but also because he desired her attention. Holding her in his arms brought happiness he never wanted to lose.

Instead of explaining himself, he joined her on the settee as if his undressing were an everyday occurrence between them. He smiled as she averted her gaze everywhere but him. He leaned back against the cushions, stretching his arm along the curve of the settee, and brushed his fingers across Sara's shoulders. His eyes lowered as her body shivered at his touch. To restrain himself from taking her to his bed this evening would require the ultimate act of willpower he'd ever possessed.

"I must confess, I had an ulterior motive in asking you to spend our time alone in our suite."

Ian's bold confession brought forth the wickedest of Sara's imagination. His gravelly tone only ignited the hunger for him to kiss her again. She didn't know how the duke held the ability to make her want to discard her inhibitions and act on her wanton thoughts, but his touch alone sent her spiraling to express her hidden desires. Her willpower to resist the passion between them slipped from her grasp with each second spent in his company.

How would she survive sharing a bedchamber with him this evening without throwing herself at him?

She took a deep breath before turning toward him. "And what might that be, Ian?"

It was on the tip of her tongue to call him *Your Grace*, but she didn't dare provoke him to kiss her. Because if he so much as placed his lips upon hers, Grace wouldn't be able to resist what she most desired.

Ian's smile turned devious. "I believe hearing my name on your lips is just as pleasurable as you calling me *Your Grace*. Oh, dear Sara, we are in a quandary indeed."

Not realizing her actions, Sara leaned closer to Ian. The pull of attraction between them was impossible to ignore. Nor did she want to. "Are we?"

Sara's husky whisper would be his undoing to abandon his quest to give her a courtship before seducing her. The desire flaring in her aqua gaze changed from the calm waves of an ocean to the stormy sea of passionate need. Why deny them what they both desired? Ian had to remind himself that Sara was an innocent maiden who deserved more than what life had granted her before they wed. His need to spoil her with the affections of a husband who loved her far surpassed his baser urges. In time, he would worship her body with his loving touch, but for now, he would show her the affections of his heart. He refused to allow his selfish urges to rule his actions.

No matter how he rationalized his thoughts, he was powerless to resist Sara. He closed the space between them and wrapped her in his arms, pulling her against him. The sensation of her pert breasts pressing into his chest drove him to spear his hands through her hair, sending her hairpins scattering around them.

He captured her soft gasp between his lips as he coaxed her to open her mouth for him. Her gasp soon turned into a moan of pleasure as their tongues tangled in a dance of seduction. Each stroke only heightened the desire to claim her as his and damn his gentlemanly intentions. He had their whole marriage to court her and shower her with his love. Making love to Sara would only show her how devoted he was to her.

Pressed against Ian as he devoured her with one kiss after another felt like heaven. She wanted this moment to last forever. She didn't believe seduction was his plan for the evening, but far be it for her to halt his attention. Especially when it sent tingles of awareness throughout her body.

She spread her fingers across his chest and up over his shoulders. From her touch, she imagined him carved from stone. Her exploration continued as she coasted her hands along his arms. Sara ached to caress his bare skin, to experience his sheer strength rippling beneath her fingertips. She dared to touch his chest where he had undone the buttons of his shirt. At his groan, she tore her hands away.

Sara stilled in his arm, unsure if she had been too forward by touching Ian in such an intimate manner. However, he entwined his fingers with hers and guided her hand back toward his chest.

"Please do not stop," he murmured in between their kisses.

His encouragement only fueled her need to discover if his skin was as soft as hers. The texture was smooth underneath the sprinkling of hair, but also hard and firm. With each glide of her fingertips, Ian moaned with what Sara now understood to be pleasure.

Her touch inflamed his senses. He wanted nothing more than to rip off his shirt and let Sara explore to her heart's desire, but his conscience warned him to slow down. His behavior was one of a scoundrel seducing an innocent miss to steal her virtue. Never mind that he was her husband and it was his right to bed his wife. But he never considered his wife giving herself to him his right but a gift. A testament to the love she held for him. He didn't need Sara to declare her love to know she did. It reflected in her gaze whenever he stared into her eyes. As much as he wanted to worship Sara's body, he needed to slow down.

His lips glided across her cheek to her ear. He groaned as her musky scent washed over him. He closed his eyes, fighting his urge to strip her bare and say to hell with his conscience. A few more kisses and he swore he would stop. He craved to kiss her delicate skin and listen to her sighs of pleasure echoing around them. When she tilted her head back as he kissed along her neck, encouraging him to continue, Ian realized he was a doomed man falling deeper under her spell.

Was it complete madness to lie entwined with her husband, who, only two days ago, was her employer? With each kiss and caress, her fantasies came to life. He rolled them over to where she lay beneath him and lifted his head to stare deep into her eyes. The passion flaring from his stare sent a rush of warmth flowing through her. His fingers hovered over the buttons on her dress. He never spoke a word but waited with his unspoken question for her permission to continue. When she slid her tongue across her lips, Ian groaned and closed his eyes as if he were in pain. But when he opened them again, they blazed with an explosive passion she never wanted to deny him.

As he did with her, she answered him by entwining her fingers with his and helping him undo the buttons of her dress. He traced a finger in a light tease across her skin above the lace of her chemise. She arched her back, aching for his touch to consume her. However, he continued to tease her by pressing kisses along the path his fingers traveled. The warmth soon turned into an all-consuming fire, with flames of need flickering inside her soul.

"Please," she begged.

Ian raised his head, his eyelids lowered with desire. "You are a tempting package. I ache to unwrap every delicious inch of you."

Sara moaned. "Ian."

"I know, my darling. 'Tis an intense yearning needing to be fulfilled. However, I fear we will spend a lifetime searching for relief we shall never find. Our bodies will only crave the next high, demanding more."

Sara couldn't respond even if she wanted to, because Ian overtook her senses when his mouth drew her nipple between his lips through her chemise. Her fingers sank into his hair, holding his head to her breasts. The ache between her thighs intensified, begging for relief. She held no clue what was happening with her body, only that she never wanted Ian to stop his seduction.

Sara clutched at him with a desperation only Ian could ease. His sweet and timid governess was a passionate woman. He found immense pleasure in teaching her how to unleash her inner goddess. He promised he would slow down, but watching her drop her inhibitions with each caress only sabotaged the best of his intentions. When she begged him, he wanted to rip her dress away and worship every inch of her. But he refused to seduce her for his own pleasure. However, he could ease the ache consuming her.

He finished releasing the buttons on her dress and drew the straps of her chemise off her shoulders. Her breasts glistened under the candlelight, and her nipples hardened under his stare. They were pale pink, begging for his lips to caress them. Ian placed a soft kiss across one nipple before moving to the next one. He licked his lips with eagerness to feast on them as he brought Sara to the pinnacle of her much-needed release. He trailed a path between her breasts, each act more intimate than the last. A lick across the tips to a gentle suck as he cupped them. They filled his palms to perfection.

He fell into a dangerous territory of being unable to stop as he suckled her luscious breasts. Sara was a divine confection, and he wanted to savor every inch of her until she appeased his cravings. But he feared he would never satisfy his lust for his wife. His hand inched lower to slide under the skirts of her dress. He ached to touch her sweetness between his fingers. Sara's legs parted for him, and she arched off the settee as he brushed his thumb across her clit. Her eyes closed in ecstasy, and a moan escaped past her lips. When he sank his fingers into her wetness, she guided his head back to her breasts in a silent request for him to continue loving her.

He drew her bud into his mouth, sucking gently as his fingers glided across her pussy, relishing the desire she held for him. His lips softened as he slid a finger inside her. Her grip tensed in his hair but soon relaxed as his finger glided in deeper. She tightened around him before her juices coated his hand. He moved his head to draw her other nipple into his mouth, increasing the pressure as his finger moved in and out of her pussy with his thumb teasing her clit with gentle flicks back and forth. He ached to slide down between her thighs and devour her wetness with one stroke of his tongue after another.

Sara lost herself in the exquisite pleasure Ian devoted himself to. She would muse over her scandalous behavior later. For now, she hoped Ian never stopped with his attention. He eased the ache as if it were a mission of dire circumstances. She hovered on the verge of falling off a cliff as his touch intensified, drawing out her desires with each slide of his finger through her wetness. His pace increased, demanding for her to soar into his arms. However, she never wanted to leap from the passion consuming her. Her body ached to become one with Ian. For him to slake her needs along with his own.

She clung to the side of the cliff as amazing ripples of desire overcame her. But when his teeth scraped across her nipple and his thumb pressed against her clit with determination for her to succumb to his pleasure, she opened her arms wide and fell into the oblivion of Ian's lair. She was a slave to his devotion. Her body floated into the abyss of his arms as he caught her to him, kissing her lips with a gentleness that bound her to him for an eternity.

"This was not my intention for the evening. However, I refuse to apologize for my actions. I would not trade this moment for anything." Ian pressed a gentle kiss against Sara's lips.

"What was your intention?" Sara asked, unable to meet his eyes.

Ian slid his knuckle under Sara's chin to tip her head up. "To spend time with my wife and plan a future with her." He gave her a wicked smile. "Maybe steal a kiss or two. Or perhaps more. I find I cannot curb my cravings for my wife's sweet kisses."

"You must think me wanton with my behavior," Sara mumbled.

Ian cupped Sara's cheek, brushing his thumb across her soft skin. "A natural act between a husband and wife as they explore their desires is anything but wanton. If so, I beg for you to behave with wanton intentions at every opportunity possible."

Sara blushed at Ian's teasing. "You are an incorrigible beast, Your Grace."

"Only for you, my duchess."

He bent his head to kiss Sara with a slow, mind-drugging kiss to show her how pleased he was that she shared his passion for them to be husband and wife in the most intimate of ways. She melted into his kiss, wrapping her arms around his neck. He rose off the settee and lifted Sara into his arms, carrying her to their bed. She would sleep wrapped in his embrace this evening and every evening for the rest of their lives. He promised she would never spend another day without feeling the love of a family.

Ian laid Sara on the bed and stripped her dress away, leaving her in her chemise. Then he moved about the suite, blowing out the candles before joining her in bed. When he pulled her into his arms, his shirt and pants brushed against her bare skin. While he seduced her on the settee with his kisses and magical touch, he'd had the most honorable of intentions with her. She wasn't that innocent of a maiden not to realize that Ian put her needs before his. His desire pressed against her backside as he held her against him. However, he held back with patience to show her how much she meant to him.

She never thought it possible, but Sara fell deeper in love with her husband.

Chapter Seven

False Rumors

SARA STIRRED SUGAR INTO her tea, oblivious to the conversation flowing around her. She fought not to blush as she remembered how Ian had awakened her that morning. His amorous attentions the past two weeks since speaking their vows kept her mind filled with the most scandalous of thoughts. He stole kisses at the most inappropriate moments and left her in a muddled state of need before she drifted to sleep. Evenings, they spent in their suite learning more about each other before their desires demanded them to explore their needs. However, each time Ian would pull back before they took their passion too far.

She longed for him to make her his wife in the truest sense. She wanted to confess her love but held back. Sara didn't want Ian to think she confused their passion for love. What she felt for Ian went beyond the attraction between them to how she viewed him as a duke, friend, father, and husband. His devotion to ease everyone's burdens only added to her adoration for him. He showed what a caring gentleman he was by including his in-laws in his decisions for Mairi. He wanted them to share his life as if they were his parents. How could Sara not love such a compassionate gentleman?

Her life grew more perfect with each passing day. They fell into a routine, with Sara giving lessons to Mairi in the mornings while Ian conducted his business. Then he would entertain Mairi in the afternoons while Sara made the rounds with Lady Whetham as she introduced Sara into society. Each day, Sara grew more confident amongst the selected group of ladies they visited. She would attend her first ball this evening. To say she was nervous was an understatement. However, Ian assured her they would leave immediately if she became uncomfortable.

Even the reason behind their marriage seemed to fade into oblivion. The villain's silence seemed peculiar, but Sara assumed her marriage to Ian threatened them to cease their taunts. Her husband was an intimidating gentleman who wouldn't tolerate anyone terrorizing a member of his family. The culprit's silence gave Sara the courage to embrace the opportunities before her.

"You are quiet today, my dear. I hope all is well?" Lady Roselli's question broke through Sara's musings.

Sara's blush deepened. "Just lost in my thoughts."

Lady Roselli softly chuckled. "I remember those days with my husband."

Sara pressed her hands against her cheeks to cool them. "You must think me too forward."

"Not at all. You are in the blush of your marriage, and I find your adoration of Somerville enlightening."

Lady Roselli's praise made Sara feel worthy of Ian's devotion. She hoped everyone saw that she'd only married Ian because she loved him, not for what his standings could offer her. She never wanted to bring shame to him or his family.

"Thank you, my lady."

"I overheard Marian mention you and the duke shall attend the Darlington Ball this evening."

Sara nodded, trying to hide her grimace. "My first official foray into society. I hope I do not embarrass the duke or Lord and Lady Whetham."

Lady Roselli tapped Sara with her fan. "Nonsense. You will only enhance the duke's standing with your beauty. Though beware of the bitter mamas and the devastated debutantes, for they will attempt to ruin your evening at every chance."

Sara frowned. "I do not understand."

"Somerville's arrival in London sent a silent statement amongst the ton of his return to society. Every family set their sights on securing a match with him and one of their unmarried daughters. However, your marriage to the duke ruined their chances, and they do not lose with grace," Lady Roselli explained.

"Oh." Lady Roselli's explanation gave Sara doubts about attending the ball. Ian had assured her the ball would be the perfect event to introduce her to society as his wife. Most of the ton had traveled to their estates in the country. Only the few remaining peers would attend the ball. Perhaps they should wait longer before attending any events.

"Do not allow those vipers to frighten you away. Stand proud next to Somerville and show your devotion to him and they will come around with their acceptance. My husband and I will be in attendance, and he is eager to meet you. I have told him all about you, and he wants to meet the lady who has helped to heal the Whetham family's and Somerville's despair."

"You have told your husband about me?" Sara asked.

"Yes. So do not disappoint my husband by not attending the festivities this evening."

Sara smiled. "It will be my honor to meet your husband."

Lady Roselli squeezed Sara's hand before rising. "Then I shall see you this evening."

Lady Roselli shared her farewell with her friends and the hostess before leaving. Sara's gaze flittered around the group who talked amongst themselves, sharing stories. The mutual affection among the friends made Sara long for her own friends. While they wrote to one another every week, Sara missed them something fierce. As she navigated this new society, she wished she could share with them her journey and ask for their advice. Vivian, Grace, and Flora were the closest she had to family, and she needed their love and support more than ever before.

Especially this evening.

False Rumors

Somerville paced back and forth in the foyer, impatient for Sara to appear. Her maid and Marian had shoved him away from their suite to help Sara prepare for the ball. When he noticed she'd tried to hide her apprehension from him, he'd wanted to ease her nervousness. She'd left with Marian for their daily socializing with excitement for the ball. However, when Sara returned, she had grown withdrawn. When he attempted to coax out her troubles, she'd assured him all was well. With one interruption after another in their preparations, Sara avoided him. It wasn't until his mother-in-law reassured him it was perfectly natural for Sara to suffer from nerves over this evening's entertainment that he ceased his worries.

He hoped the surprise he had waiting for her would help to soothe her tensions. However, her surprise would also raise unanswered questions. He had avoided telling Sara the truth he had discovered about her parents. Ian risked the fragile state of their relationship with his neglect of not being honest with her. No matter how he tried to rationalize his excuses, he would be at fault for hurting Sara.

"If you do not stop your pacing, you will portray the wrong message to your wife," Stuart remarked.

Somerville turned toward his father-in-law. "What would that be?"

Stuart pointed his hat at Somerville. "That you are ashamed of her."

Somerville glared at Stuart. "I hold no shame for my wife, and I resent your accusation."

"Calm down. I am only stating how Sara might perceive your pacing. She is already worried she might shame us. You need to show how calm you are to reassure her."

Somerville swiped his hand along his face at his thoughtlessness. Stuart was as wise as ever. He had always taken his father-in-law's advice, and this situation was no different. When Sara glided down those steps, he needed to wait for her with eagerness to show off his new bride. She didn't need to see his nervousness. He wasn't anxious about her shaming him or what the gossipmongers' opinions were. He worried her evening wouldn't be the success she deserved.

Ian nodded his understanding at Stuart. He moved near the stairs with his hands behind his back and waited for Sara and Marian to descend. His father-in-law joined him, patting him on the back with reassurance that the evening would be a success.

"Ah, there are the gems of the ball," Stuart complimented as Sara and Marian walked down the stairs arm in arm.

Marian left Sara and slid her hand through her husband's arm. "Still as charming as ever, my love. But the only gem this evening is our dear Sara. Does she not look lovely?"

"Like a fresh rose that has bloomed under the sun's attention." Stuart winked at Sara.

Sara blushed and dipped into a curtsy. "Thank you, my lord. Your sincere compliment warms my heart."

Stuart chuckled. "Sincere and truthful."

Marian swatted at Stuart. "I told you, Sara, to be aware of my husband when he turns on the charm."

Stuart brushed a kiss across his wife's cheek. "Someone has to charm the poor girl. Her husband behaves like a smitten suitor who is bumbling in his attempt to charm her."

"Oh, Stuart. Cut the boy some slack. He's never had to charm a wife before." Marian guided Stuart away to give Sara and Somerville time to themselves.

Sara's appearance struck Somerville speechless. When she appeared at the top of the stairs with her hair billowing around her shoulders and her dress molded to her soft curves, he wanted to tear up the stairs, sweep her into his arms, and carry her back to their suite. The turquoise gown only highlighted the depth of her ocean-filled eyes, bringing out the sparkle of Sara's personality. The gown left her shoulders bare and cupped her breasts with its design. He must keep her near his side this evening to scare away any scoundrel who would dare to approach her.

Sara patted her hair and smoothed the sides of her dress. Ian's silence sent a fresh wave of nervous energy through her. Was there something wrong with her appearance? Had he changed his mind about attending this evening's festivities? She wished he would speak.

"Ian," Sara whispered.

Somerville raised his head from his perusal and noticed Sara's apprehension. "Forgive me, my dear. Your beauty has left me dumbfounded and unable to function as a proper gentleman."

He must work on his charm. He no longer bumbled; instead, he rambled on with ungentlemanly manners and perused his wife like a scoundrel. His behavior was shameful at best, and he needed to be reprimanded. Since his in-laws had given them space, he needed to control his baser urges and offer Sara the assurance she needed before they left.

He stepped forward and lifted her hand to his lips, kissing her knuckles. "I apologize for my crassness. You are a vision I cannot wait to have stand by my side this evening."

Both of his compliments sent a tide of warmth rushing through her to settle in her soul. They held a charming nature that eased her insecurity and gave her the courage to attend her first social event as Ian's wife. While people would clamor for her attention because of her title, she wanted them to like her for her personality alone.

"I hope I do you justice."

He wrapped his arm around her waist, drawing her against his chest. "You far surpass it, Sara. I could not be prouder of you and the courage you display by accompanying me this evening. However, I fear we cannot leave until you finish your attire."

Sara glanced along the length of her, trying to see what she might've missed. Marian had helped her dress for the ball. "I am confused what I may have forgotten."

Ian released her and picked up the jewelry box from the table against the wall. He opened the lid to display a necklace with a turquoise stone surrounded by diamonds lying on a strip of velvet. "A background adornment to enhance your beauty."

Sara coasted her fingers across the gorgeous stone. "I cannot."

Ian ignored her protest and clasped the jewelry around her neck. It lay nestled on her chest, dipping between her breasts. The diamonds were perfect, glistening against her pale skin. The diamonds were the first of many jewels he would spoil her with. What made Sara so worthy of them was that she never expected them and would cherish the gifts he bestowed upon her.

"You can."

Ian never gave Sara a chance to voice her objection. He pulled her back into his embrace and took her lips under his in a slow gentle kiss, expressing what he held in his heart but being too much of a coward to tell her. It was the perfect moment to share his love, but he allowed his dishonesty to keep him from exposing his heart to Sara. He only wanted the truth between them when he declared his feelings. His lies would only confuse her when she learned the secret he held.

Sara gave up her resistance to the treasure Ian gifted her. He pressed his mouth against hers in a silent message, declaring himself with an unspoken confession. With each pull of his lips, Sara clutched at him and returned his kiss with her own silent message. She wanted to declare her love but worried he didn't reciprocate the depth of her feelings. While she'd promised to attend the ball, she wanted nothing more than to spend another quiet evening in their bedchamber lying in each other's arms. Only tonight, she wished for Ian to make love to her.

A throat cleared from behind them. "I see you recovered your ability to charm your wife. However, I fear I must disturb your amorous attention to encourage you to join us in the carriage. The Darlington Ball awaits your presence," Lord Whetham teased.

Sara pressed her head against Ian's chest in embarrassment. "Your father-in-law must think me most wanton with my behavior."

"Stuart only teases you because he finds you a delight," Ian reassured Sara.

"My behavior is scandalous," Sara disagreed.

Ian kissed the top of Sara's head. "Your behavior shows my in-laws your devotion, and they find joy in our happiness. Now, shall we make our appearance? I believe this evening will be a success in more ways than one."

Stepping away from Ian, she pressed her fingers against the diamonds and made a silent wish that Ian's belief extended to when they were alone in their bed. The evening had started on a magical note when she walked down the stairs and saw the lust and adoration shining in Ian's gaze. His every action showed Sara his devotion to sharing his life with her.

How could the evening not end with the magic of love?

Chapter Eight

False Rumors

Silence swept across the ballroom floor at their entrance. Then the hushed whispers echoed around them when Ian wrapped his arm around Sara's waist in a scandalous gesture of possession and protectiveness. Married couples of the ton never showed affection toward one another, and they frowned upon a couple remaining by each other's side throughout a ball. However, Ian never let Sara wander away from him, and she declined each offer of a dance. She wasn't skilled on the dance floor and refused to show her ineptitude to those who might find fault with her. Her lower class was enough of a default, and she refused to give them any more reason to gossip about their marriage.

A countless stream of people demanded their attention throughout the evening, with introductions that left Sara exhausted. However, she kept her practiced smile in place and pretended an interest in their tiresome discussions. She longed for familiar conversations with her friends, who weren't full of false pretense or having to listen to society's overinflated egos. She pleaded her excuse, whispering her need to visit the retiring room to Ian. Sara didn't give him time to accompany her before slipping into a throng of guests passing by them.

Instead of the retiring area, she slipped into a room quiet from the festivities. The library was aglow with candles and a fire crackling in the hearth.

Sara turned around in a circle, admiring the vast collection of books. The library was even more impressive than Ian's. Her fingers trailed across the tomes and she quietly whispered the titles. She wished nothing more than to select a book and curl up in a chair and lose herself in a story. Sara preferred the make-believe worlds to the one she now found herself in. She fought to shake off her guilty thoughts but failed with the truth of them.

Sara sighed at her conflicted emotions. She didn't want to fail Ian but worried she was incapable of emerging into the lifestyle needed to be his duchess. If everyone this evening were of the quality she had met on her visits with Marian's friends, she believed she would find success. However, the quality of people she'd met this evening didn't share the same characteristics.

"I could not agree with you more, miss."

Sara stilled at the bookcase when she heard the gentleman's voice. She had thought she was alone with her thoughts, but it would appear she had invaded someone else's privacy. When she turned, an older, distinguished gentleman was sitting in the corner with a book on his lap. He hadn't hesitated to enjoy himself as he pleased. Oh, how she envied him.

Sara cleared her throat. "I apologize. I never meant to intrude."

He gestured for her to take a seat. "You haven't. It seems we shared the same idea to steal away for a peaceful moment."

Sara settled on a chair a distance away. "Perhaps for longer if I am allowed."

"Is the ball not your idea of a pleasant way to spend your evening?"

Sara winced. "If truth be known, I would much prefer to replicate your actions."

He laughed. "I would think someone of your beauty would have her dance card full and a line of smitten suitors paying her attention."

Sara blushed. "My husband would not be agreeable to such attention."

"I apologize, my lady. I presumed you were a debutante who did not want to please her mama and preferred books over courting."

Sara smiled wistfully. "I fear I never knew my mother."

The gentleman grimaced. "It would appear I am stepping on my own toes with you this evening."

Sara's smile brightened. "Quite the opposite. I find our conversation most refreshing from the others I have had this evening."

"The lot can be most pretentious, and that is on a decent day."

Sara smoothed her hands along her skirts. "I fear for them on a grave day."

He set the book on the table next to him. "Most ferocious."

Sara chuckled in response. She should have left the minute the gentleman spoke, but his honest conversation was the first one she'd enjoyed all evening. If anyone were to walk in on them, it would cause rumors to spread about Somerville's new bride already seeking the attention of another gentleman. Even though it was a harmless visit by two people who wanted to escape and clear their minds before rejoining the overwhelming guests who preened with their insincerity amongst themselves.

"I thought I might find you in the library and entertaining a pretty lady too," a familiar voice interrupted them.

Sara rushed to her feet to show nothing untoward had happened. "Lady Roselli, 'tis you."

"Yes. I see you have met my husband."

Lord Roselli rose. "Informally, my dear." He bowed to Sara. "It is a pleasure to meet the legendary Sara. My wife sings your praises daily."

"You are a lucky gentleman, Lord Roselli. Your wife is a dear who has welcomed me into her fold. I am honored to call her a friend."

Lady Roselli clapped. "I am thrilled you two have met. Now, to convince her to join us for tea soon."

Lord Roselli slid the book back into place on the bookshelf. "That is an excellent idea. We shall send an invitation to Somerville next week. Shall we rejoin the ball, my love, and allow Sara a moment to collect her thoughts in private?"

Lady Roselli glanced back and forth between Sara and her husband, pleased they had met and appeared comfortable with one another. "Yes. Enjoy your evening, my dear. We shall be in touch soon."

Sara watched the Rosellis leave the library and frowned at the lord's swift departure with his wife. They had enjoyed an amicable visit until Lady Roselli arrived, and then the lord had appeared out of sorts with the situation. His behavior confused Sara because nothing untoward had happened. Perhaps she had misinterpreted his reaction. After all, it had been a stressful evening attempting to understand everyone's intentions.

She glanced back at the bookcase, wishing to indulge in her greatest pastime. However, she must return to Ian's side before he searched for her or whispers started about her disappearance. With one last glance, she ventured back to the ballroom to find Ian. He was easy to spot, because a crowd stayed gathered around him, striving for his attention. Sara had observed this evening how his absence amongst the ton had held a resounding impact.

Once Sara wandered to his side, he slipped his arm around her waist, giving it a light squeeze all while continuing his conversation. He soon finished and guided Sara to the dance floor. He nodded at the orchestra to play a song. After all, he was a duke, and everyone jumped to do his bidding. Soon, the soft melody of a waltz drifted through the ballroom, and Ian swept her in a dance that left her breathless from his attention. His gaze stayed fixed on hers through every dip and turn. Her heart quickened at the intimacy of the dance, and his hold on her filled her imagination of them making love.

She needed to reel in her scandalous thoughts, but Ian made it impossible when he brushed her hair off her shoulder and bent to whisper in her ear. "You are an exquisite sight, and I missed you by my side."

Sara tipped her head back to gaze into his eyes. "I am sorry. I needed a moment alone."

He pressed a kiss against her ear. "Did it help?"

Sara gasped at his intimate display of affection. "Your Grace, you must restrain yourself."

"I fear I cannot when you are near."

Sara closed her eyes as he glided them around the ballroom floor. He was shameless with his seduction for all to watch. "I beg you to stop."

Ian chuckled. "If you insist, my love."

Sara's heart stopped at his endearment, then started again with a rapid beat. He couldn't possibly mean to call her his love. She read too much into the affectionate term. "I do."

The music ended, and the other dancers wandered away, leaving them alone. Ian drew Sara's hand through the crook of his arm. "Are you ready for your surprise?"

Sara's brows crinkled in confusion. "Surprise?"

Ian didn't answer but kept walking them toward the corner of the ballroom where the Whethams conversed with a group of ladies and gentlemen. There were too many people in front of them, blocking Sara's view. When they reached them, the Whethams stepped away for Sara to see the guests they were visiting. She almost burst into tears when she saw Vivian, Grace, and Flora standing side by side with their husbands. Each of them wore a warm smile to greet her with. Sara rushed at them, and they encircled her in their arms for a heartfelt greeting, laughing with joy at her reaction.

Sara swiped at the tears leaking from her eyes when she gazed back at Ian. "My surprise."

His humble nod set Sara to release the floodgates of her happiness on her friends' arrival. She didn't care what a soul thought of her as she hugged and kissed Ian for everyone to see. She would deal with the repercussions of her scandalous act later. For now, she wanted to express her gratitude at how much he pleased her.

"Enjoy your surprise, my love." Ian kissed her cheek before sauntering away with her friends' husbands and the Whethams.

"I cannot believe you are here." Sara gripped Vivian's hand.

"Come, love. Somerville has arranged a private room for us to visit." Vivian led Sara to a lovely sitting room nestled away from the ballroom.

Sara sat next to Vivian on the settee, while Grace and Flora sat across from them with a table between them. Once they settled in their seats, a maid poured them each a cup of tea.

"That will be all," Vivian informed the maid.

After the maid left, Grace arched an eyebrow at Sara. "My love?"

Sara shook her head. "'Tis only a term of endearment, nothing more."

Flora frowned. "That was not the impression I noticed."

Sara avoided her friends' gazes and murmured, "Then you misinterpreted."

Flora smirked. "No. I do not believe I did."

Sara sat her teacup on the table. Flora's teasing flustered her. How could she explain the state of her marriage to her friends? They were each madly in love with their husbands, who doted on them with love and affection. Her marriage resulted from her need for protection. Even though she longed to ask them for advice, it was too personal of a topic to discuss. However, who else could she ask, if not her friends?

"Flora," Vivian warned.

Flora shrugged. "I am only stating the obvious."

Grace laughed. "And in doing so, you have made Sara uneasy."

"No," Sara disagreed. "She is only voicing her opinion of something I am unsure of myself."

Vivian set her tea down too. "We are here to offer our support. Somerville wrote to us, asking us to visit because he sensed you needed your friends. Has it been difficult to adjust to your role of duchess?"

Sara smiled. "Quite the opposite. Lady Whetham has taken me under her wing to help guide me into society. I make the rounds with her daily, and her friends have welcomed me into their group."

"And Somerville?" Grace inquired.

A fresh shade of pink blushed across Sara's cheeks. "He is, um..." Her gaze darted away. "That is ..." She attempted to clear the lump in her throat. "We have not ..."

Vivian patted Sara's hand. "We understand."

Sara's breath whooshed out of her in a very unladylike manner. "I wish I did."

Grace fluttered her hand in the air. "Then you have not?"

Sara gave a slight shake of her head.

"Oh." Grace sighed.

Flora's lips twisted to the side. "Has he not even tried?"

Sara kept her head down, too embarrassed to meet her friends' eyes. "We have been intimate. But not in the full sense."

"Do you wish to?" Vivian asked.

Sara nodded.

"'Tis simple. You shall seduce your husband this evening," Flora declared.

Sara gasped. "I cannot. I would not even know how to."

Grace's smile turned secretive. "You will not have to do anything."

Sara frowned. "I am confused."

Grace took a sip of tea, prolonging her reply. "'Tis simple really."

Vivian rolled her eyes. "Please do not keep us in suspense."

Grace glanced at Flora for help with her explanation. "When you retire to your bedchamber this evening, ask him to help you undress."

"He will find it impossible to resist you," Flora added.

"And if he does?" Vivian asked.

"Then Sara must become the seductress. It starts when we rejoin our husbands in the ballroom," Grace explained.

"The kiss you bestowed on him for all of London to see was an excellent start," Flora stated. "Now you must continue with soft gestures of affection. A touch on his sleeve. Entwining your fingers with his. A whisper in his ear."

Sara pressed her hands against her cheeks. "I cannot be so bold."

Grace relaxed back in the chair. "I believe you can."

Sara looked at Vivian for guidance. Her friend had been silent while the others encouraged her to seduce her husband with wanton attention. Vivian smiled her encouragement for Sara to pursue what her heart desired.

Sara smiled at her friends. "I have missed you, ladies. Thank you for leaving your homes and families to be here for me."

Vivian hugged Sara. "We are family, dear Sara. We want to offer our support for you during this transition, as you have for us in the past. Also, we have brought our families with us."

"The children?"

Grace rose. "Yes. So we must meet at the park tomorrow because the children have missed Mairi."

"Oh, she would love to see them. She has missed them too," Sara exclaimed.

Flora wiggled her eyebrows. "While they play tomorrow, you can tell us if our suggestions worked."

"Flora," Vivian and Grace reprimanded.

Flora hooked her arms through Sara's and walked with her back toward the ballroom. "They act like they are prim old married ladies, when they are anything but. They secretly want to know if Somerville will fall for your charms. My money is on he will. A husband does not stare at his wife the way Somerville does if he doesn't desire her in his bed. He is more than eager to claim you as his."

Flora had always been the more outspoken of them and never hesitated to speak her thoughts. Sara wished she had half the courage Flora did at approaching life. Perhaps she could channel Flora into being her inspiration and take her advice. In the end, what did she have to lose? She wanted a marriage in the truest sense with Somerville. One where they expressed their love and made decisions with one another. One without secrets or fears haunting them. She wanted to have his children and make a home with him.

Once they reached the ballroom, they found their husbands in a deep discussion. However, the men stopped talking once they arrived and each of them whisked his wife to the dance floor, leaving Sara and Ian alone. She expected Ian to place his arm around her waist as he had all evening. Instead, he wrapped her in his embrace and smiled down at her.

"Did you enjoy visiting with your friends?"

"Yes."

He pressed a soft kiss against her lips, and everything faded away in the background at being held in his arms. It was as if they were the only ones who existed. And nothing or no one else mattered but them alone. They would be the talk of the town tomorrow with their scandalous behavior, but Sara didn't care. Perhaps her friends were correct about how Ian felt about her.

Hopefully, she would discover soon.

Chapter Nine

False Rumors

Somerville followed Sara up the stairs to their suite, fighting the urge not to sweep her into his arms and carry her to their bed. He had already been presumptuous when he informed her maid that he would see to his wife's needs on their return. The past two weeks had been the sweetest torture he had ever endured.

He could no longer resist making Sara his.

He desired his wife with a passionate need that pushed him to the point of no return. He could no longer deny himself what he had wanted since he first laid eyes on her.

His thoughts the past few hours had taken a wicked twist with each press of her breasts against his arms to the soft caresses she tempted him with. At first, he'd thought they were innocent gestures to catch his attention, but the desire blazing from Sara's eyes spoke otherwise. With boldness, she whispered in his ear about how she eagerly awaited his kiss before bed. Was his sweet-natured wife seducing him?

Sara paused on the top step. With a shy smile over her shoulder, she held out her hand to him. Their fingers entwined as they had countless times throughout the ball, but this time, Sara's fingers tightened around his as they entered their suite.

Once they neared the bed, Sara dropped his hand and turned her back on him. "Will you undo my buttons?"

Ian needed no other encouragement from his bride. He stepped forward and brushed Sara's hair over her shoulder. He trailed his finger along the length of buttons keeping him from her succulent skin. Ian refused to rush a second of this with his demanding urges. His desire to savor Sara with slow precision would only enrich their experience. His hand trailed upward until he reached her neck. He bent his head and pressed his lips against the softness.

Sara shivered at Ian's touch, aching for him to undo her dress. However, he teased her with his patience. She lowered her head as his lips trailed a path from the back of her neck along her bare shoulders. He continued his seduction with each button he released, burning a path down her back.

"Step away," he whispered in her ear.

Sara obeyed Ian's demand and stepped away from her dress. Even without her friends' encouragement, Sara had planned her seduction when she dressed for the ball. She hadn't worn another stitch under her dress except for a pair of stockings clipped around her thighs. She had hoped to entice him to abandon his resistance and make love to her. His indrawn hiss behind her flooded her senses as he gripped her bare hips and brought her flush against his front. The evidence of his desire pressed against her, leaving Sara on the verge of begging him to make love to her.

Sara closed her eyes as she gathered the courage to become a bold seductress. She slowly turned in Ian's embrace and pressed her hands against his chest. The rapid beat of his heart gave her all the encouragement she needed to continue her seduction. Her fingers made quick work of undoing his cravat and the buttons on his coat and vest. She peeled them off his shoulders, and they dropped to the floor next to her dress. Sara lifted her gaze and lost herself in Ian's fiery expression. He held the look of a man possessed with need, one who held himself back from unleashing his passion on his desired subject.

She wanted nothing more than for him to lose control of his inhibitions. To break away from his proper behavior and allow his wicked desires to consume them. She ached for Ian to control her with his baser needs. Sara was no longer the proper governess, nor did she want to be the proper duchess inside their bedchamber. She wanted them to explore the passion that ruled the attraction between them.

Sara reached for Ian's hand on her waist and brought it to her breast. His eyes darkened with an unspeakable need as he brushed his thumb across her nipple and pinched it between his fingers. She shifted to rub her thighs together at his intimate touch. Her ache had intensified to an unbearable need she desired for him to ease.

"Duchess," Ian moaned.

Sara's tongue darted out between her lips. "Yes, Your Grace?"

Her teasing reply would be the downfall of his intention to slow their lovemaking until he savored every one of her hidden delights. However, her tongue sliding against her lips and her body naked before him broke what control he fought to hold. Sara was a seductive minx beneath her innocent façade. She made it impossible for him to restrain himself a second longer. And why should he? She was his wife. So why shouldn't he make her so in the truest sense of their union?

Ian bent his head to draw her nipple between his lips and suckled the berry until it tightened into a hard bud. Sara's moan echoed around him when he licked around the bud, teasing it before moving to the other nipple to savor its sweetness. He ached to sample every inch of her and listen to the melody of her pleasure echo around them.

Sara's knees gave out at Ian's intense devotion to loving her. He caught her in his arms and laid her on the bed. At one time, his bold stare would've had her covering herself. Instead, she only felt more desirable. He tore at his shirt and kicked off his trousers until he stood before her as a man whose only purpose this evening was to make love to the woman he most desired.

Sara.

Her gaze raked his form with a hunger only he could satisfy. His muscles rippled with his unrepressed need to touch her, and she ached for him to unleash his desires. Her gaze trailed lower to where his hand stroked the length of his cock. Soon she would feel the strength of him inside her, pulsing with his need alongside hers. Her fingers curled into the quilt to keep herself from reaching for him. Her inexperience left her doubting if she held the skills to seduce her husband.

Ian dropped to his knees when doubt filled Sara's gaze. His hands glided along the smooth silk of her stockings. She was bewitching, wearing not a stitch but those. When he reached the garter, he placed a kiss on each flower pressing against her thighs. He eased her legs apart and grazed his thumb across her glistening clit. Sara arched her back off the bed at his touch. Her gaze no longer held doubt, but desire flared from her turquoise depths.

His wife ached for his love, and he would spend an eternity worshipping at her feet if she would forever gaze upon him with love shining from her eyes. Silk caressed his sides as he pressed himself between her thighs. He blew a soft breath against her core, causing Sara to lift her hips.

"Ian," she moaned.

Ian smirked before sliding his tongue along her pussy. "Yes, Your Grace?"

Her husband not only teased her with his reply but left her incapable of any coherent thought with his attack on her senses. Her fingers uncurled from the blanket and sank into his locks as he trailed a path of fire across her wetness with his tongue. With each teasing flick of his tongue, Sara lost herself in the passion and succumbed to his wicked pleasure. They no longer held themselves back from the attraction demanding them to be together. They were free from the polite demands of their union. Now they were two souls binding themselves together with the passion in their souls.

One taste of Sara and he drowned in the erotic flavor of her on his lips. Her musky scent inflamed his senses to draw her desires to pinnacle heights with each caress of his tongue. Every night since they married, he'd introduced Sara to the pleasure of intimacy while staying dressed. His wildest fantasies had never prepared him for the exotic lady he now pleasured. She was far more delicious than he had ever imagined.

He set a rhythm, sliding his fingers in and out of her pussy, while his tongue flicked against her clit with an intensity to send her into a frenzy of release. But as soon as her pussy gripped his fingers, he pulled back and licked her with slow strokes, drawing out her release, only to repeat the act. Silk rubbed against him with each slide of her thighs pressing tighter against his face. With each lick of her wetness, he hungered for her release. He not only tortured Sara with his teasing but himself too.

He gripped her hips and brought her flush against his mouth. With each slide of his tongue seducing her to succumb to their desires, he urged her to move her hips in rhythm. He no longer wanted to deny them her pleasure. Soon her hips raised and pressed against his mouth as her body shuddered with her release. Her wetness coated his tongue, and he devoured Sara like a starving man hungered for her sweetness.

Ian kissed a path up Sara's body, devoting himself to her pleasure. He lit a fresh fire in her with each gentle caress and soft kiss. While he eased her ache, he built a need inside her that left Sara breathless. As he rose above her, she reached out to grip his arms and wrapped her legs around his waist. She waited with eagerness for him to make her his. It would hurt, but she welcomed the discomfort for the chance to become his wife. His lover. His soulmate.

And hopefully one day his love.

Ian held back from sliding his cock inside Sara. The passion surrounding them pushed him to the edge of controlling himself with her. He needed to enter her gently to ease her discomfort. However, the need coursing through him demanded its fulfillment. Once the warmth of her pussy wrapped around his cock, he would be powerless to slaking his desires with the intense ache racing through his body.

He slammed his mouth against hers, ravishing her lips with a kiss that left them both breathless. He gathered her in his arms as her fingernails dug into his shoulders, and with a slowness he didn't believe himself capable of, he slid inside Sara. She tensed for a second as he pushed past the slight barrier of her maidenhood, but soon sighed into their kiss as her hands caressed the length of his back. Her gentle touch would be his salvation from taking her like a savage.

Sara melted into Ian's arms as he slid in and out of her with a gentleness that brought tears to her eyes. Her white knight made love to her with a care that made her dreams come true. However, Sara soon discovered she much preferred the untamed passion her knight kept hidden behind his shield. Now, only to entice him to indulge in his wicked desires.

His wife's seductive smile as she teased him with a kiss should've been a warning that he would lose the last of his control. He lost himself in the pleasure of her lips as she trailed a path of kisses along his neck and across his shoulders. When she arched her back, he swore she scraped her nipples against his chest to tease him. But when she rotated her hips before wrapping her legs around his waist, he realized he was powerless to resist her spell a moment longer.

"Duchess," he warned.

"Yes, Your Grace." Sara's laughter teased him.

He pressed in deeper and held still. "You are playing with fire."

"Then burn me," Sara whispered in his ear.

Her taunt, along with the brush of her hands gripping his buttocks, sent him over the edge. His demure governess shared a dark need with him that only he could fulfill. He caressed her hips as he slid from her warmth. The tip of his cock hovered at her entrance, building their anticipation to fly over the edge together.

Sara attempted to press forward, but Ian held her firmly, withholding the pleasure their souls desperately craved. The storm gathering in his gaze kept her entranced under his spell. She was but a willing slave to their impending passion. She gasped when he pushed his cock inside her with a powerful thrust. Before she drew another breath, he repeated his act, deeper than before.

His thrusts became more demanding as his tongue licked at her nipples. He bit them with a softness to appease his hunger. No part of her was untouched by his reckless passion. Each caress singed her and left her aching for more. She felt herself spiraling, lost in the ecstasy of their lovemaking.

Ian roared as he exploded inside Sara, and she tightened around him with her own release. She clung to him, lost in the rapture of their souls joining as one.

He rolled over, bringing her across his chest while they caught their breath. He never meant to take Sara with such force her first time, but he'd abandoned his morals once she tempted him with her seductive expectations.

When Sara pressed a kiss against his chest and her fingers traced a path back and forth across his stomach, Ian tightened his grip on her hair. She decided to embrace her wanton thoughts and entice her husband to make love to her again. Her lips trailed higher to his, and she gave him a gentle kiss, enjoying the press of his mouth against hers.

He pulled back. "You are impossible to resist."

"Then why try?"

Why indeed? Ian brought his mouth back to hers and continued their kiss. Each pull of their lips became more demanding as their passion raged out of control again. Soon, he rolled them over and entered Sara with the fierceness his soul demanded. His wife matched his need with her own uncontrollable passion.

They were a match destined for eternity.

Chapter Ten

False Rumors

SOMERVILLE HELD THE PARCHMENT up to the sliver of moonlight shining through the bedroom window. He didn't want to light a candle and awaken Sara. He needed to be alone with his thoughts and deal with the guilt consuming him. It'd been his intention to share his secrets before he made love to her. However, he had been powerless to deny the passion between them for a second longer after Sara tempted him with her innocent seduction.

His gaze drifted to the bed where Sara lay against the bedsheets with her arm flung above her head. The sheets wrapped around her curves in a tangled mess, barely covering her breasts. He fought to crawl next to her and wake her with his kisses. The hunger for his wife was all-consuming now that he'd savored her sweetness. However, he held back while he tried to understand the cryptic message that had been delivered to him during the ball.

A secret has been revealed.

What secret? And to whom? He had yet to understand this madness steeped in secrets. Ian feared if he informed Sara what he'd learned about her past, he would place her in danger. The secret of her birthright made her vulnerable to people who would harm her. He would do anything in his power to protect her. Even from the two souls who'd lost all privilege to Sara once they discarded her to protect themselves from judgment. She was an innocent who didn't deserve the treatment dealt to her.

"Ian."

Ian raised his head to see his wife had risen onto her elbows, the sheet dropping from her breasts. When she held out her hand for him to join her in their bed again, he stuffed the letter into the pocket of his robe and strode to her side. She reached out to tug at the belt on his robe, and he shook it off before wrapping Sara in his embrace. Her soft sigh as she melted against him pulled him under her spell. She had been an enchantress this evening and one he would no longer deny himself.

He lost himself in their kiss, forgetting the confusing message. Tomorrow, he would deal with the villain who cruelly tormented them. For now, he only wanted to love his wife.

The precious lady who held his heart.

False Rumors

Sara stretched as she awakened from her dream and winced at the tenderness between her thighs. Then she remembered it wasn't a dream but a wonderful memory of Ian making love to her. She turned her head to find him, but the bed was empty except for a rose and a letter lying on his pillow. A smile of pure happiness graced her face at his thoughtful gesture. She lifted the rose and inhaled the flowery scent as she read his note.

Come join me for breakfast.

Sara tossed off the covers and jumped from the bed, eager to see her husband. Most would call her excitement shameless behavior for a lady of her standing. But she didn't care as long as she spent time with Ian. She rushed around the bedchamber, getting ready in one of her new dresses and styling her hair down with the sides pinned back.

Sara paused and took a deep breath to slow her racing heart. She needed to calm down before she left their suite. How she behaved in privacy differed from how she must conduct herself under her peers' and the servants' observation. She refused to give them any reason to slander her character and bring shame to Ian.

That left her noticing the tangled bedsheets and their clothes strewn across the floor. Ian had forbidden any servants in their chamber unless requested. They were only to clean daily once Ian and Sara occupied themselves elsewhere. He did so at her request because she was unused to servants waiting on her when she had been one herself only recently. She must adapt to the hierarchy of her station. However, the current arrangements suited her for now. Once they returned to Scotland, she would accept her position as a duchess by following the routine deemed for her.

Sara hurried around the bed, tugging the sheets and blanket into place. She laid their clothes on the bed for the servants to take care of. In her hurry to prepare herself for Ian, she had dropped his letter. When she bent over to retrieve the parchment, she noticed another letter had slipped out of the pocket of Ian's robe. It was the size of a calling card with only a message slashed across its surface.

A secret has been revealed.

She turned the card over, searching for any sign of who it might be from. But the other side was blank. Secret? Sara frowned at the confusing message. Had the villain struck again? If so, it differed from his usual letters filled with taunts and slanderous words. Since their wedding, the culprit had remained silent. Why hadn't Ian shared this with her?

She bit her bottom lip with indecision. Should she leave the card and pretend she never saw it? Or should she take it with her when she met with her friends later? Sara didn't want to risk Ian's ire at stealing his personal business. But her curiosity about what the card could reveal prompted her to slide it inside the pocket of her dress. Her friends would know how to handle the card. Also, they had seen enough of the villain's handwriting to decipher if it was from him. She had only ever received one letter and had since given it to Ian. While more letters had arrived, Ian was the intended victim to terrorize. Her husband never shared them with her in his effort to protect her.

While she found comfort in his protection, it left her vulnerable to the culprit's vengeance. Her friends had also kept the truth of the culprit's cruelty from her, assuming she was too naïve to handle the truth. She must prove to those who loved her the strength she held to fight against the vengeance aimed at her.

Starting today.

Sara stepped out of their suite at the same moment a maid led Mairi from her bedchamber. Mairi dropped the maid's hand and ran to Sara in a very unladylike manner. She fought to hold back her chuckle at the servant's disapproving stare. Sara knelt and held her arms out for Mairi. When Mairi snuggled into her embrace, she forgot about the mysterious card.

"Did you dance at the ball, Momma?"

Sara's smile brightened. "Yes. Your father twirled me around the ballroom floor. It was a magical evening."

"I want to dance at a ball with Poppa."

Sara laughed. "One day you shall. However, for now, would a visit to the park to play with your friends from Scotland please you?"

Mairi pouted. "We cannot. They are too far away."

Sara tapped Mairi on the nose. "No. They have come to London to play with you."

Mairi jumped up and down before grabbing Sara's hand. "Hurry, Momma, we must eat breakfast so we can play in the park."

Mairi tugged Sara to the breakfast room in her excitement. She would have to curb her enthusiasm once they returned to Scotland, or else she wouldn't grow into a proper lady but a heathen. However, for now, she allowed the child the freedom to adjust to the changes in her life with Sara's marriage to Ian. The girl emerged from her shell with the rambunctiousness of a child curious about everything. And she never wanted to repress Mairi's need to discover new experiences.

Mairi rushed to Ian and crawled onto his lap. She held her hands against his cheeks to get his attention. "Did you hear, Poppa? All my friends came to play with me."

Ian winked at Sara before focusing his attention on his daughter. "Yes, I heard. You have some very special friends."

"I know."

Ian laughed at her simple declaration and glanced at Sara to see her staring at them with a fond expression. When she met his gaze, her smile turned shy with a blush gracing her lovely cheeks. However, Ian was now well aware of the temptress she hid behind her innocent smile and couldn't wait to discover more of Sara's hidden desires.

He rose and rested Mairi on the chair next to him. Then he sauntered toward his wife, enjoying how her blush darkened from pink to red. He drew her into his arms, brushing a kiss across her lips.

"Did you sleep well?"

"Mmm," Sara replied, swept away by how Ian dominated her senses.

Ian chuckled. "I will take that as very well."

Sara pressed her head against his shoulder to hide her embarrassing reaction to his nearness. "You may."

"Perhaps I can show you another bedtime ritual tonight you will enjoy, to help you sleep," Ian murmured in her ear.

"Your Grace."

"I warned you, my love, about calling me *Your Grace*."

Sara gave him a warning glare that was anything but frightful.

"It only urges me to kiss the words from your lips to hear you sigh my name instead."

Her tongue darted out to lick her lips in anticipation.

Ian groaned. "You are a walking temptation that causes me to lose myself in front of all those around us."

Sara rose to her tiptoes and brushed a kiss across his cheek. "Then perhaps you should restrain yourself from your teasing."

Ian chuckled at her impish reply as she moved away to sit on the other side of Mairi. While he would've preferred her to sit next to him, he realized his wife held more sensibility by keeping them apart. It only pleased him that Sara suffered from the same ailment. Unable to resist one another.

He rejoined the table and listened to his daughter's excitement at seeing her friends soon. While he preferred for them to play in the townhome gardens, he refused to steal Mairi and Sara's usual ritual from them. Their visits to the park in Scotland, where Sara had introduced Mairi to other children, had drawn his daughter out from the sorrow she'd suffered since her mother's death. While Mairi was too young to hold memories of her mother, she experienced her loving presence every day of her life. Once Claudia died, the loss of her mother's love impacted her greatly. Love Sara restored with her tender nature. Not as a replacement, but with its own string of memories.

Ian would provide protection while they enjoyed their visit. No one stood the chance of harming them. This would allow him to meet with Courtland, Lockhart, and Hepburn to discuss what he'd discovered about Sara from his investigation and the message he'd received the evening before and what their insight might be.

While Sara enjoyed his daughter's animated conversation, he was the one to watch them with fondness. The Whethams had slept in, exhausted from attending the Darlington Ball. So it left them in an intimate family setting. In Scotland, Sara had refused to join them for meals and either ate with the other servants or in her bedchamber. He never got to watch his governess and daughter together as a family. It was a sight to behold. Nothing or no one would ever sever the bond between them.

Sara was his to protect.

Chapter Eleven

False Rumors

Mairi tore off to join her friends once they stepped out of the carriage and she spotted them playing nearby. Sara followed at a leisurely pace to the benches where her friends sat. She didn't need to hurry after Mairi to keep her safe when she noted Ian's and the Whethams' servants scattered around the area. Their presence had made her uncomfortable when she first arrived in London and when they increased after she became Ian's wife. However, she understood her husband's need to keep them protected, and she never uttered a word of protest. Not when it gave her the sense of security that he cared enough to see to her welfare.

While he never professed his love, she wasn't blind to see he cared about her by the tender gestures he bestowed upon her. Their passion had raged out of control, but underneath the fierce dynamics of their desires, there was a gentleness to each kiss and caress he seduced her with. His promise at breakfast left her eager for nightfall to arrive.

"The blush blooming across her cheeks shows proof that her evening ended in success," Flora quipped.

Grace joined in with the teasing. "Well, I noticed she took our advice to heart throughout the evening."

"The question is if it continued once she got Somerville alone in their bedchamber," Flora wondered.

"Ladies, please show Sara the respect she deserves as a duchess," Vivian reprimanded.

Grace smirked. "Always playing the lady, dear Vivian, when we are well aware you are stewing with curiosity yourself."

Vivian lifted her chin with an elegance Sara always admired as she declared, "Perhaps so. However, I hold the dignity of refraining myself from invading Sara's privacy."

"Bollocks," Grace and Flora burst out before clutching at each other in laughter.

Vivian shook her head in rebuke. "Sara, please sit while we suffer from their tomfoolery."

Sara tried to hold back her amusement but failed, especially when she noticed the twinkle in Vivian's gaze. Her friends' enjoyment at her expense was a welcome balm to the whirlwind of emotions she had endured since Ian asked her to marry him. While her emotions still overwhelmed her, she had learned how to handle them.

Her friends waited with patience for her to reveal how her evening had ended. They didn't expect any crass details. However, curiosity sparkled from their gazes to learn if Sara got what her heart most wanted.

Ian's love.

She could wait to hear his declaration and offer of his heart again. His late wife's death had broken him, and he still needed time to heal. Time she would grant him.

"The evening ended in success."

Their squeals of joy echoed around Sara. Their excitement made their friendship special in her heart. Her friends only wanted the best for one another. She had met them at her lowest. Now her life was full of the love of friendships and family.

Vivian tilted her head to the side as she observed Sara. "Did he declare his love?"

Sara shook her head.

"Ah, love," Grace murmured, reaching out to squeeze her hand in sympathy.

Sara offered them a wistful smile. "'Tis fine."

Flora pinched her lips. "I never thought the duke a foolish gentleman."

Sara's smile widened at her friend's defense. "Not foolish but a gentleman still suffering from heartache. He will come to love me when he is ready."

"As he will. How could he not? You are his dream come true," Grace declared.

"Aye," Flora agreed.

"It warms my heart how confident you are in Somerville. However, I can tell something else troubles you this morning," Vivian commented.

Vivian had always been the more insightful one in their group, as well as the one to develop a plan whenever they were in trouble. She had been protective of them since their first meeting when they welcomed her with offers of friendship. Because of her, they had met and married the gentlemen they now loved with all their hearts.

Sara withdrew the card from her reticule and handed it to Vivian, who read the message and passed it to Flora and Grace. Sara didn't understand their confused reactions.

"This slipped from the pocket of Ian's robe this morning," Sara explained.

"Did you question him?" Vivian asked.

"No."

"Do you have any clue what it might mean?" Grace questioned.

"None. I hoped one of you might recognize the handwriting."

Flora scrutinized the card, running her fingers along the script. Her expression changed when she recognized the handwriting. "'Tis him."

Sara gasped. "Are you certain?"

Flora handed back the card. "Aye. The penmanship matches the letters the villain sent to Lennox."

"'Tis what I feared. But what does the message mean?"

Vivian glanced at the children, keeping her expression hidden. "Has Somerville spoken with you about what he discovered about your past?"

"No."

Vivian swung her closed-off gaze toward Sara. "Perhaps you should question him."

Sara frowned. "Do you know something?"

When Vivian didn't answer her, Sara looked at Flora and Grace, who both avoided her gaze. It hurt her feelings that her friends kept secrets from her. Not only her friends but Ian too. Did her friends hold her husband's opinion that she was too fragile to learn the truth about the threats that centered on her?

Sara pinched her lips and clutched her hands. "I see."

Their visit had taken a turn from animated enjoyment to their betrayal that stabbed Sara's heart. While she had hoped for their support to decipher the cryptic message, they had kept secrets from her, ones that could help her understand the mystery behind the threat that plagued her every day.

Sara rose from the bench and called for Mairi. "Come along, love. Your Poppa is waiting for us."

Sara detested lies but found it necessary to escape the uncomfortable situation with her friends. Their loyalties lay with their husbands and what they might've confided in them. But to keep secrets that profoundly affected her showed Sara their friendship, and her marriage to Ian, was nothing more than a façade. In truth, she only had herself to depend upon.

"Sara, please don't leave. Allow us to explain," Vivian pleaded.

Sara turned with a false smile to protect herself. "'Tis unnecessary. Thank you for allowing the children to play with Mairi today. It has brightened her spirits. She has missed her friends."

Sara didn't allow them to respond but gathered Mairi and hurried to their carriage. She felt terrible for tearing Mairi away from her playmates, but she couldn't handle another moment with her friends. Mairi never complained, though, only exclaimed over playing with her friends at the park, oblivious to Sara's pain. As she should, considering her age. Sara never wanted Mairi to be aware of life's injustices.

When they arrived at the Whethams' townhome, Sara sent Mairi with a footman and waited until they stepped inside the house before directing the carriage driver to a destination she hadn't visited since she arrived in London. They would report her activities to Ian, who would expect an explanation upon her return. But for now, she needed to visit her favorite spot, where no one would bother her with her thoughts.

The carriage pulled up to the shoppe nestled between two housing structures. It was a place she had discovered when she missed home. Sara had found comfort in browsing the shelves. The shopkeeper had enjoyed her visits and offered her a room abovestairs, where she could curl up with a book and enjoy a pot of tea to escape her loneliness. She'd never told anyone about this place. Her secrecy of the bookshop would keep anyone from finding her for a while.

When she opened the door, the bell rattled, indicating her arrival. The few customers in the shoppe glanced toward the door, then redirected their interest back to their search. An elderly lady hustled around the counter toward Sara. When she reached her, Mrs. Hardy pulled Sara into a motherly hug. Sara wrapped her arms around the portly woman and found comfort in the genuine affection.

Mrs. Hardy held Sara away from her and eyed her up and down. She nodded in approval. "I heard news of your marriage."

"Shh," Sara interrupted her.

She didn't want the other customers to overhear her connection to Ian. She wanted to be Miss Sara Abbott for a few hours, not the Duchess of Somerville. Mrs. Hardy nodded her understanding and hooked her arm through Sara's, leading her to the new arrival section.

"Pick out a book while I find Mr. Hardy to watch the shoppe. Then we can have a friendly visit over a pot of tea. I have missed your sweet face." Mrs. Hardy hurried away.

Sara perused the titles, hoping to find something that would help her escape her troubles for the afternoon. She wanted to forget the past few months of terror and how her husband and friends had betrayed her with their secrets. Her rash behavior to disappear was out of the norm for her. However, at that point, she no longer cared. She wished to avoid the false-hearted behavior always directed at her.

Sara grabbed a book at random and moved to the counter. Mr. Hardy rang up her purchase. He was a quiet gentleman who allowed his wife to entertain their customers with her exuberant knowledge of literature.

As always, he offered her a kind smile. "Your return has thrilled the missus."

"I have missed our visits," Sara confided.

"As we have with you. Hurry, before she exclaims to the customers what you hope to avoid with your visit," Mr. Hardy warned.

Sara nodded and hurried to the back of the shoppe where Mrs. Hardy waited to lead her abovestairs to their set of rooms. She followed her up the stairs and curled up on the sofa like she always had before she left for Scotland. Mrs. Hardy carried a tray toward her, and Sara sat forward, clearing a spot on the table. She set about to pour the tea when Mrs. Hardy waved her to sit back, and she covered Sara with a blanket. The motherly gesture soothed her wounded pride a little. Mrs. Hardy handed her a cup of tea before sitting across from Sara with her own cup.

"What troubles you, my dear?"

Sara sipped at the warm brew. "I have never felt so alone."

"Why do you believe that?"

That was what Sara admired about Mrs. Hardy. She offered no false assurances because of Sara's circumstances. She reminded Sara of her grandmother by always being available for advice and ready to help Sara carry her burdens. It was Mrs. Hardy she'd run to when her employer, Lord Baldridge, had attempted to accost her. Then when Lord and Lady Baldridge dismissed her without pay or a reference and she struggled to find employment, Mr.

and Mrs. Hardy had offered her a room. She'd never shared with her friends how she survived during those trying times.

"Because my husband and friends are keeping secrets that affect me."

Mrs. Hardy nodded. "And you know this how?"

"They more or less revealed the truth today during our visit to the park."

"Perhaps if you start at the beginning, I might have a better understanding of your troubles and can help you," Mrs. Hardy suggested.

Sara set the teacup down and pulled the blanket tighter around herself as she snuggled into the sofa. She began by telling Mrs. Hardy about the threatening letters she and her friends had received over the past year. Then she told her about the lady at Flora's ball who'd informed Sara that she should return to Fordwich. She ended her explanation by describing how Ian had only married her to offer his protection. Mrs. Hardy only interrupted with questions when needed and then she grew silent again for Sara to continue.

She shared how she had fallen in love with Ian and thought he returned the sentiments from how he treated her. Sara finished with the card she'd found this morning and the conversation she'd shared with her friends. The retelling of their betrayal caused tears to coast down her cheeks. She swiped at them, and Mrs. Hardy handed her a handkerchief. She sniffled into the fabric and brushed it across her cheeks to dry her tears.

"It is my opinion your friends withheld the truth because they believe your husband should be the one to tell you his secrets, not them," Mrs. Hardy offered.

In her rush to get away from them, Sara hadn't stopped to consider the predicament she'd placed them in. Obviously, Ian had confided in her friends' husbands, and they had shared the information with their wives, who they didn't keep secrets from. It hadn't been fair of her to place them in an awkward situation. However, their silence only gave Sara doubt about their friendship, especially when she only ever offered them honesty. Was it too much to expect equal treatment?

"As for the duke, 'tis his role as your husband to fulfill his duty to protect you."

A fresh set of tears came to Sara's eyes. "I do not wish to be his duty. I only want him to love me."

Mrs. Hardy joined Sara on the sofa, wrapping her in her arms. "Oh, my dear, if your husband did not love you, he would never protect you. I have heard of marriages amongst the aristocracy where husbands neglect their wives and do not care if their wives come to harm. You are among the fortunate whose husband would go to any lengths to keep you out of harm's danger."

Sara sniffled. "Ian does not love me, nor will he ever. He only offered marriage to protect me because he does not want to lose me as a governess to his daughter."

"Oh, Sara, you have no clue of your value. It would be an impossible feat for the duke not to fall in love with you. I believe the duke realized what a rare treasure you are and found it impossible to resist making you his wife."

Sara frowned at Mrs. Hardy but never disputed her comment. She couldn't deny Ian's attraction to her from how he'd taken her with passion the night before. However, his inability to trust her with what he'd discovered caused her heartache. Her lack of knowledge of the facts caused her a loneliness she couldn't explain.

Mrs. Hardy stood and adjusted the blanket around Sara. "Take a while to gather your thoughts. I must not leave Mr. Hardy alone too long with the customers."

"Thank you," Sara whispered.

"All will be well, child. You must have faith Somerville has only the best of intentions toward you."

Sara watched Mrs. Hardy bustle away before stretching her legs out and turning on her side. She thought over her situation and what actions she should take on her return. Her disappearance this afternoon would cause Ian distress. She wished she had the courage to confront him but worried her reaction would disappoint him. Their marriage was too fresh to cause disruption, especially when Ian only held the most honorable of intentions regarding her welfare.

Perhaps she should give him the benefit of the doubt and wait for him to confide in her. If he didn't, then she was left with no other option than to inform him that she wouldn't wait for him to decide about her welfare without her opinion. To do so might cause friction in their marriage. However, she'd learned from her friends' marriages that, without honesty, they were destined for a marriage of discontentment.

Sara threw the blanket aside and moved to the mirror to fix her appearance. She needed to return to the Whethams' townhome before Ian sent out a search party for her. She preferred for him not to learn of the bookstore she sought refuge in when life became too difficult for her to understand. One day, she would divulge how Mr. and Mrs. Hardy had taken her in when she needed them most. If the duke was allowed his secrets, then the duchess was allowed hers too.

Sara slipped down the stairs and down an empty aisle. Before she took another step, someone rushed around the corner, knocking into her. She dropped her book and reticule. When she bent over to retrieve them, someone grabbed her elbow.

"Allow me," a gentleman offered.

Sara took a step back to shake off the improper hold and winced when she noticed the person who had knocked into her was Lord Roselli. A kind gentleman who had no other intention than to help her. Her troubled thoughts had misinterpreted his actions.

"Thank you," Sara murmured when he handed over her items.

He tipped his hat. "My pleasure. 'Tis wonderful to see you again, Your Grace. Or may I call you Sara?"

"I should not allow it. 'Tis most improper."

"Are you not a friend of my wife?"

Sara nodded.

"Then, as her friend, you are mine too. And friends call each other by their first names," Lord Roselli attempted to persuade Sara to see his reason.

Sara glanced around the shoppe. "Perhaps in private we can be less formal."

"Excellent. Have you found a book to purchase?"

Sara clutched the book to her chest. "I already have. I was on my way out."

Lord Roselli offered his arm. "Then allow me to escort you. 'Tis an unpleasant section of London for you to wander without an escort. Anything untoward might happen to you. I would never forgive myself if you came to harm."

Sara laid her hand on his arm. "Thank you. I appreciate your generosity."

Sara searched the front of the shoppe as they walked toward the exit. She had hoped to thank Mrs. Hardy for her kindness. But neither she nor her husband was anywhere to be found. She would send them a letter on the morrow with her gratitude.

Lord Roselli escorted her to her waiting carriage and helped her inside. "Until we meet again, Sara. It was a pleasure to see you today."

He clicked the carriage door shut and slapped the side, directing the driver to leave before Sara could respond with her farewell. The intimate way he spoke her name sent a strange shiver throughout her. Was it foolish of her to allow him to call her by her Christian name in a private setting? After all, her friends and their husbands allowed the familiarity.

Sara leaned her head back against the seat cushion, exhausted by what was proper or improper conduct. Why couldn't it be as simple as when she was a governess? The lower class could be themselves and be honest with their actions. The deceit among the higher class had Sara wishing for simpler times. But then, she would never have shared her life with Somerville.

Why was life so unfair?

Chapter Twelve

False Rumors

Somerville paced across the study in a worried state. Sara hadn't returned with her friends as planned. Instead, she'd had a footman walk Mairi into the townhome before she left in the carriage to an unknown destination. Her friends had no clue where she might've gone to gather her thoughts. Now the hour grew late, and Sara still hadn't returned. He didn't know where to search for his wife. He hoped Sara remained with his men to protect her.

He stopped to stare at her friends. "Was she upset enough to leave?"

"London?" Grace asked.

Somerville nodded.

Vivian rose and placed her hand on Somerville's sleeve. "No. She would never leave you and Mairi. She only needs time to herself to process what she believes to be our betrayal."

"There is no belief, 'tis the truth," Flora mumbled.

Vivian frowned at Flora to stay silent. "She is confused."

"No, she is not," Flora argued. "She is upset that we have left her in the dark by the secrets her husband keeps."

Hepburn squeezed Flora's shoulder. "Easy, lass. The duke had his reasons for not sharing the truth with Sara."

"And what reasons were those, Somerville?" Lockhart demanded. "Because of your secrecy, you have placed our wives in the middle of your marital issues."

The room grew quiet, with everyone attempting to accept the part they played in keeping secrets from Sara. 'Twas no use blaming one another when the only importance was finding Sara. Her disappearance was unlike Sara to cause anyone to worry about her.

"Did you become familiar with Sara's activities when you lived with her after we lost our positions?" Vivian asked Flora.

Flora frowned. "Sara and I shared no lodgings together."

Vivian's eyebrows drew together. "I thought you had. You two always arrived and left the park together."

"Only because we arrived at the same time. I assumed she stayed with a family member or friend once Baldridge dismissed her," Flora explained.

"Sara has no other friends than us. And her only family had been her grandmother," Grace stated.

"Perhaps if we knew where she lived, we might know where to search," Courtland mused.

The ladies stared at one another, unsure where Sara might be. Caught up in their troubles, they had neglected to learn more about their friend. They did not differ from Somerville by protecting Sara instead of helping to guide her through the difficulties of life. They had failed her. Instead of refusing to reveal Somerville's secrets, they should've helped her understand their stance and encouraged her to speak with Somerville. They were as much at fault as Somerville in causing her disappearance.

"Your Grace." The butler stood inside the entryway.

"Yes, Simmons?"

"The duchess has returned."

Somerville stepped forward. "Please inform her I wait in the study with her friends."

"I have already done so. She offers her apologies, but she has retired to her bedchamber for the day. Also, a message has arrived for you." Simmons handed the letter to Somerville.

"That will be all, Simmons."

The butler left, and Somerville tore open the letter without seeing who sent it. Anything to escape the awkwardness of Sara's dismissal toward him and her friends. He'd placed her friends in a difficult position by sharing his findings with their husbands and caused a rift between them and Sara. He needed to follow their leads and share his information with his wife. If he'd been honest since they spoke their vows, then they wouldn't be suffering through this discord. Ian needed to explain to Sara what he'd discovered about her past and encourage her to forgive her friends. He must face her disappointment and seek her forgiveness.

Somerville,

Your wife is such an exquisite creature. I had the pleasure of enjoying another conversation with her this afternoon.

Tsk, tsk for not watching your wife more carefully.

Perhaps she is best left under my care.

Until next time ...

Somerville snarled. "That bastard has met with Sara."

Grace gasped. "How? Where?"

Courtland peeled the parchment from Somerville's hold. He read the letter and then passed it to the other gentlemen. "He has escalated his threat by presenting himself to Sara."

"More than once, it seems," Lockhart commented.

"He implies he has spoken to her before today. Do you know when?" Vivian inquired.

"No. She has either been in my company or Lady Whetham's since we married. It must be recent or else he would have taunted me before now."

"Did she leave your side at the ball?" Flora asked.

"Only to use the retiring room. She was not gone too long before you arrived," Somerville explained.

Vivian frowned. "Sara uses that excuse to escape from the festivities. The aristocracy causes her unease, and she would suffer now more than ever. She probably escaped to the library for a spell. Did she mention meeting anyone new?"

Somerville shook his head. "No."

Lennox showed his wife the letter. "Have you learned who the initials stand for?"

Somerville dragged his hand through his hair. "No. My investigators have had no luck either."

"You need to confess to Sara about what you have learned. Since the clues involve her, she might remember something that could help solve who is behind the threats," Vivian suggested.

Lockhart stood and held out his hand to help Grace rise. "Until you do, then we are unable to help. Speak with Sara, Somerville. You are no longer a duke and she your governess. She is your wife, and therefore, you need to treat her as such."

The couples exited the study, leaving Somerville alone with his thoughts. If any other gentleman had spoken to him with such authority, he would've dismissed him from his home. However, he had developed a friendship with Lockhart, Courtland, and Hepburn, as well as their wives. Lockhart had spoken out of respect for their friendship.

He should follow their advice and talk with Sara now. However, he was too much of a coward to see disappointment clouding her gaze. He wouldn't lie to himself not to admit that her admiration of him had inflated his ego to where he only wanted to be her knight in shining armor. To protect her from all harm. Instead, he had failed her faith in him with his deception. And in doing so, he had placed her in the villain's path.

Somerville strode from the study to search for Simmons. He needed to ask the carriage driver and footmen where they took his wife. Also, it was pertinent he learned who she'd come into contact with. Once he learned this information, he would share his secrets with Sara. Hopefully, once he confessed the truth, she would understand and forgive him.

False Rumors

It was discourteous for Sara not to greet her friends and their husbands. To play the gracious duchess to Somerville's astute duke. However, exhaustion had taken hold from pretending her life was perfect, when it was anything but. Her emotions had taken their toll for the day. She only wanted a hot bath to relax and an evening spent on the chaise reading one of her favorite books. She wished to escape from the real world into a story of fantasy. Tomorrow she would deal with Ian's deception and her friends' betrayal.

Sara had placed her request with the butler and then checked with the maid caring for Mairi. When she entered the bedchamber, she noticed the tub filled and a tray left by the servants. She only hoped Ian would keep his distance while she gathered her thoughts. While a visit to the Hardys' bookshop had helped, she still hadn't forgiven everyone for their deceit. More than a few simple apologies would allow her to trust Ian and her friends again.

Sara nibbled on a sandwich as she dipped her fingers into the water to test the temperature. Since it was too hot, she ate and drank the tea. After she finished, she toed off her shoes and undressed. She twisted her hair into a bun before sliding into the water with a sigh. She laid her head back, closing her eyes. The warm water wrapped her in a cocoon of comfort.

Why must life be so difficult?

She must have fallen asleep for a spell. Her lids rose from her lazy slumber to see her husband standing above her with a look of desperation and regret.

He had stripped himself bare except for his trousers. Ian knelt on the floor and wrapped his hand around her neck, bringing her to him for a kiss.

The kiss was gentle, begging for forgiveness. With every nip, his kiss grew more desperate for her to respond. His tongue stroked her lips apart and slid inside to tangle with hers in a dance of slow seduction. Sara was powerless to resist the attraction between them. She succumbed to his kisses, winding her arms around his neck. She should demand for Ian to release her, but to do so would deny herself the pleasure she desperately needed to feel loved. Their lovemaking spoke what they both were too scared to admit.

Ian rose and lifted Sara from the tub without breaking their kiss. He laid her on the bed with a tenderness that brought tears to her eyes. He discarded his trousers and slid next to her, bringing her into his embrace as if there were no troubles between them. Only a husband wanting to love his wife. The silence between them would be a divide, but it was one they ignored to explore the pleasures of the flesh. Their attraction was no longer an issue now that they were husband and wife. However, it was a hindrance when they used it to lure them away from their troubles.

But one Sara was incapable of denying.

He was a selfish bastard for kissing Sara instead of seeking her forgiveness. Her vulnerability was a temptation he couldn't resist. His desperation for her to return his kiss led him to dominate her senses by staking his claim. Making love to her wouldn't solve their problems, but his frantic need for Sara's offer of forgiveness pushed him to seduce her.

He trailed a path of kisses down her neck, along her shoulder, down to her breasts, kissing away each drop of water from her body. He licked at her nipple before drawing the bud between his lips and softly sucking, savoring her sweetness. Soon her fingers sank into his hair, guiding him to her other breast. Repeating his actions brought forth a sigh of pleasure from Sara.

His lips followed the path of his hands, caressing every inch of Sara's curves. Her petite frame held many dips and valleys for him to worship. Her thighs parted for him at his silent command when he teased her clit with his thumb. He avoided her every attempt to touch him. Ian feared Sara would demand for him to cease his lovemaking. He needed to show her how much she meant to him. He couldn't lose her too.

Sara had sunk deeper under Ian's spell not to pull away from him. He set a fiery path across her body with each kiss he caressed upon her. She ached with a need to feel loved, and Ian soothed her heartache with each kiss that reached her soul. At his soft touch against her core, she parted her thighs, needing him to close the divide between them with his kiss.

If she thought his lovemaking would be tender to plead for her forgiveness, then she was mistaken. Their passion grew uncontrollable when he slid two fingers inside her pussy while he devoured her wetness with each wicked lick. He ravished her like a man starved for salvation. His unrelenting attention left her at his mercy.

With each stroke of his fingers, her need built, begging for release. She fought to call out his name and beg him to soothe the fire consuming her soul. But her heartache kept her silent. Instead, she rotated her hips to match the rhythm of his fingers, pressing her core to his face with her own demands to reach the heights of pleasure she ached for. Waves of bliss washed over her at once, catching her unaware.

Sara shook beneath him from her release. He should relent with his determination, but desire ruled his actions. The feelings he held for Sara left him wandering in unchartered territory. He felt her heartache deep in his soul. Instead of wrapping her in his arms and confessing his secrets, he continued his onslaught of seduction. He rose above her and slid his cock inside her with a slowness that had him holding his breath until her warmth surrounded him as he settled deep inside her.

When Ian entwined his fingers with Sara's, her eyes fluttered open to stare deeply into his. The heartache gazing back at him seared his soul with an agony too indescribable to understand. He bent his head to kiss away the single tear that slid down her cheek. Her reaction should've been warning enough for him to confess his love, but he held back from making amends. He had no excuses for his behavior. Instead, he captured her lips in a soul-searing kiss while he made love to her with tender care, expressing his love with each slow stroke in and out of her body.

Sara closed her eyes, unable to bear the agony of staring into Ian's eyes. His depths held a tortuous storm of emotions that left her unsure of what he held in his heart. She couldn't deny the passion or the protective nature of his tender touch. However, his other feelings were too difficult to decipher without understanding her own tortured emotions. Instead, she lost herself in the hunger consuming them, with each joining of their bodies as one. His fingers tightened against hers as if he pleaded with her to open her heart to him.

However, the events of the day had left Sara too vulnerable to open her heart to Ian. She didn't deny she loved him, but she couldn't say the words until she understood the reason for his actions. Since she met him, his behavior had been one contradiction after another. Would he ever open his heart to her? Or would their attraction fade away?

Ian sensed that Sara waged a battle with her reaction to him. However, her body couldn't deny the bond between them. They glided in a slow dance of seduction with each whispered sigh of satisfaction. She arched against him as her pussy tightened around his cock. Ian could no longer deny them the release their desires demanded. He slid out slowly, only to thrust back inside as deep as he could to reach Sara's soul, and their bodies exploded with the passion neither of them could deny.

Ian gathered Sara into his arms and held her close to his heart, never wanting to let go of her. He held no clue how to proceed. How did he explain to his wife that his deception was rooted in how she shook his very foundation? That his love for her made him want to be the husband of her dreams? Was he capable of such a feat?

As much as Sara wanted Ian to speak about the secrets between them, she didn't want to spoil the haze surrounding them from their lovemaking. So she stayed silent, hoping Ian would too. Her eyes drifted closed as she relished his soft caress through her tangle of hair. His soothing gesture soon relaxed her enough for her to drift off to sleep.

Tomorrow was soon enough to share their secrets.

False Rumors

Ian followed the sound of his wife's and daughter's laughter to the nursery. Sara had risen before him, leaving him to awake alone in their bed. Before he fell asleep, he'd thought to wake before her and deliver breakfast to their suite for them to share an intimate conversation. As he held Sara while she slept in his arms, he'd realized what a fool he had been by never revealing how much he loved her.

In his effort to protect his heart from never getting hurt again, he had caused Sara a heartache he had never wanted her to experience. Life was unpredictable and out of one's control. Her disappearance yesterday made him aware of how precious his love for her was and how he needed to express the depth of his emotions for her, along with the secrets he kept from her. By keeping his secrets, he left her vulnerable to the bastard terrorizing them and had caused a disagreement between her friends.

Ian leaned against the doorjamb, watching Sara and Mairi, who were oblivious to his arrival. Sara sat across from Mairi in her robe, eating a breakfast of scones and jam. Her hair lay in tousled disarray around her shoulders, making her far lovelier than the hairstyles her maid insisted on when she accompanied Marian on their outings. Her bare feet peeked out beneath her robe, causing Ian to realize he much preferred this version of Sara to the one she must present as his duchess. He couldn't wait for their return to Scotland, where he planned to surprise Sara and Mairi with a visit to his estate in the Highlands. There, they could be themselves, not what they must present to society.

He smiled as Sara licked off a spot of jam from the curve of her thumb. She tapped Mairi on her nose as his daughter giggled at their mess. His daughter's happiness was music to his ears. Each day, her sadness faded away with the joy of Sara in her life.

"I do not know who wears more jam, you or the table," Ian teased.

"Silly Poppa. The table cannot wear jam."

Ian knelt to his daughter's level and kissed her forehead. "Silly me. Now that I have gotten a closer look, I can see my mistake. It is most definitely you who wears the jam. I thought you were to eat the jam on your scones?"

Mairi giggled. "Momma and I think the jam tastes more delicious all by itself."

Ian's gaze slid to Sara, who bent her head to avoid him. "Does she now?"

Ian's soft murmur caused Sara's heart to race. She had slipped away from their bedchamber to escape their conversation. She had been unable to resist him the evening before when he kissed her with such tenderness in the bathtub. Nor when he loved her with a gentleness that caused her heart to weep with the uncertainty of their marriage. She was a coward to face their troubles, afraid Ian wouldn't respond to her questions with the truth.

"Try it, Poppa," Mairi insisted.

"I think I will." He slid into the chair next to Sara, pressing close to her.

Sara inwardly groaned at the proximity of their chairs. The furniture in the nursery was designed for children, not adults. His thigh pressed against the thin material of her robe, searing her with his warmth. If she dared to move away from him, he would see the effect he held over her with his innocent presence. Her hand fluttered against her robe to close the gaping opening.

Ian fought to hide his smile of satisfaction at seeing Sara flustered by his presence. Since she didn't leave him to be alone with his daughter, she must be open to airing the rift between them. He wasn't foolish enough to believe their lovemaking had solved their problems. However, her reaction to his closeness showed he had a chance at earning her forgiveness, which he planned to achieve as soon as he finished spending time with his daughter and Sara together as a family.

He dipped a spoon into the jam and brought it to his lips to enjoy the sweet treat, when Sara shook her head in disapproval. He frowned, lowering the spoon.

"No, Poppa! That is not the way." Mairi shook her head, her curls bouncing around.

"How else am I to try it?"

"Like this." Mairi dipped her finger into the jam and licked it off.

Ian tilted his head in question at Sara. She rewarded him with an impish smile and then surprised him by scooping a chunk onto her finger. She slid her finger inside her mouth and closed her eyes as she sucked the sweetness away. Her moan almost caused him to embarrass himself.

Ian cleared his throat. "Ahh, like this?"

Sara bit back a smile when Ian grimaced as he dipped his finger into the slippery jam. She covered her mouth to hold back her enjoyment as his first attempt ended with the jam falling down his shirt front, staining the white fabric with a red glob of stickiness. His next attempt fell on the table. But his third attempt ended with him sucking the jam off his thumb in an act that brought forth the most scandalous of thoughts. She gulped at the desire flaring to life in his eyes. It would appear her husband's thoughts held the same wickedness.

Mairi clapped, pulling their focus away from each other. "Now you are the messy one, Poppa."

Ian chuckled. "So I am. But I know how to change that." He dipped his fingers into the jar and touched Sara's and Mairi's noses at the same time with the confection. "Now we all match."

They erupted into a round of laughter that strengthened their bond as a family. They spent the next hour making memories Sara would cherish for an eternity. It was then she realized Ian's intentions. He kept secrets to protect those he loved. He may not love her, but he cared about her. Of that, Sara felt deep in her soul.

Two maids entered the nursery to clear away their breakfast. Sara lifted Mairi into her arms and kissed her, whispering in her ear. Mairi hugged Sara before Sara handed her over to the maid to bathe and dress for the day.

Once the maid carried Mairi away, Ian grabbed Sara's hand. "Can we talk?"

"Yes."

He squeezed her hand. "In the library in an hour."

Sara nodded her acceptance. She didn't trust herself to say anything more. His gentle approach left her feeling a vulnerability that made her unsure of the outcome of the conversation they would have.

Ian walked Sara to their suite and left her at the door with a gentle kiss on her forehead. He wanted nothing more than to follow her inside and gather her in his arms. To hold her while he confessed his secrets and love to her. In his neglect, he had failed to fulfill his promise of courting her because his greed to make her his had dominated his every action. They needed to have an honest discussion without their attraction distracting him from making amends.

He owed Sara the truth.

Chapter Thirteen

False Rumors

SARA REACHED THE THRESHOLD of the library to find Ian waiting for her with a bouquet of white tulips clutched in his hands. The poor stems showed signs of falling off under his fierce grip. She had seen Ian in a range of emotions since she met him, but she had never seen him nervous. He held out the flowers to her with a smile that held a hint of boyish charm. Oh my, her heart had no chance but to succumb to the mere magnetism of Ian Somerville.

Sara lifted the bouquet to her face to inhale the heavenly scent. "Thank you," she murmured.

Ian bowed before offering his arm to walk her to the settee. She laid the bouquet on the table and slid out a single tulip to hold on her lap. Ian stepped away from her and walked to the fireplace, putting distance between them. She frowned at his behavior, wondering why he'd appeared excited when she arrived and grew aloof now. However, when he ran his hand through his hair, she noticed him shaking. Their conversation was just as important to Ian as it was to her.

"I appreciate you agreeing to speak with me."

Sara slid a petal between her fingers. "We are husband and wife. 'Tis inevitable we discuss the issues between us."

Ian started to pace back and forth in front of Sara. "True. We are ... Though what I mean to say is ..."

His inability to form a coherent answer caused another wall to crumble around Sara's heart. She took pity on him and the sincerity of his attempt to make amends. She held out her hand. "Ian."

Ian came to a halt at Sara's outstretched hand. The patience in her gaze gave him the courage to accept her offering and settle down next to her. He refused to relinquish her hold. To do so would allow his fears to take control of the situation and cause him to blunder his attempt to win her heart.

"I do not know where to start."

Sara entwined their fingers together and laid them on her lap. "Wherever is the easiest to begin."

"When we arrived in London, I hired a private investigator to look into your past. I hoped to uncover a connection between whoever has terrorized you and your friends the past year. The investigator unveiled a lead concerning your parents."

Sara frowned. "My grandmother never spoke of my parents. Only how they abandoned me to her care when I was a babe. She refused to discuss them because she never wanted me to feel unloved. When she passed away, I found nothing in her belongings to show who they might be."

"Your grandmother was a clever lady who kept you protected from your parents. I learned she moved you to Fordwich and resumed a new identity so your mother could never use you as a pawn in her quest to gain entrance to society," Ian explained.

"I do not understand."

Ian shifted to face Sara. "Your mother had an affair with a married gentleman who was a prestigious lord of power amongst the ton. When he learned of his mistress's pregnancy, he demanded she rid herself of the child. However, your mother refused. Instead, she left town to return to her mother's home, where she gave birth to you. When the lord learned of your mother's deceit, he tracked her down and bribed her with money and jewels to keep her silent. It wasn't long after that your mother abandoned you with your grandmother. Your grandmother knew your mother would return one day to use you to blackmail your father whenever she needed more coin."

Ian paused to allow Sara to absorb the truth about her parents. "So she moved away so her daughter could never find you, where you spent your life until she passed away. She thought her secret was safe. However, your grandmother neglected to understand how your father had tracked her every move through the years. He knew the exact moment when you arrived in London."

"Who is he?" Sara whispered.

"There lies the mystery. Your grandmother left a journal with a neighbor. The journal held details of your birth and your father's initials. Your grandmother confided the truth to her neighbor for your protection. She feared if anything happened to her, the authorities would leave you in an orphanage. She wanted the neighbor to contact the lord to prevent that. However, the neighbor is now quite elderly and can't recall the lord's name. She only had the scratching of his name on a faded piece of parchment."

"And my mother?"

Ian caressed her wrist in a soothing motion. "She vanished, never to return."

Sara took a deep breath to fight back her fear of the question she needed to ask. "Do you hold the opinion my father is the person behind the threatening letters?"

"Yes, I believe so."

Ian's honesty left her astonished at how someone who should've loved and protected her would be the same person who'd frightened her friends and now threatened her. She wanted to weep at the injustice. However, it wouldn't solve the dilemma before them. She needed to show Ian her strength for him to realize she wasn't a fragile miss who couldn't handle the brutality of what life offered. Yes, she'd had a loving grandmother who'd protected her, and now her husband offered her the same protection. However, in the attempt for her to never come to harm, they'd left her naïve to the danger surrounding her.

"Are my friends and their husbands of the same opinion?"

Ian hung his head. "Yes."

"Did you demand for them to keep your secret?"

Ian gripped Sara's shoulders. "No. It was never my intention for them to betray you. I shared my findings with Courtland, and he informed Lockhart and Hepburn on his return to Scotland. I never expected them to share the discovery with their wives. Though I should have known better. My only excuse is how you have consumed my every thought. I neglected to understand the dynamics of what a marriage should be. When your friends arrived yesterday and made their disappointment known, I realized I had failed you."

Sara's eyebrows pinched together. "But you were married before."

Ian sighed. "My marriage to Claudia differed as night and day to the one I share with you."

Sara stayed silent as Ian rose to pace again, attempting to gather his thoughts about how to describe the differences between their marriages. Marian had already spoken of a few disparities, but only Ian could describe how the connections differed. She leaned back against the cushions as she patiently awaited his explanation.

Ian sat on the edge of the chair with his hands hanging between his legs as he attempted to articulate his thoughts on how to describe his marriage to Claudia without causing Sara any doubt that he loved her. He would confess his love after he explained the differences.

"Our parents arranged my marriage to Claudia when we were babes and nurtured by friendship. Claudia never wanted to understand the trivial aspects of being a duke, and she expected me to make every decision in our marriage without her consideration. I took on the role, believing that was how all marriages conducted themselves. She was my best friend but never my confidant. I had only ever considered my counsel until I met you and your friends."

"That experience must have come as a shock to you," Sara mused.

Ian attempted a smile. "An unforeseen experience. However, the more conversations I share with the gentlemen, the more I discover what having a friend entails. Our discussions about the threatening letters have been insightful, to say the least."

Sara frowned. "However, not enough for you to confide in me."

"I thought I was acting in your best interest if you never heard the truth about your birthright. In my attempt to protect your feelings, I failed to consider how my secrets would come between us. I apologize, my love, but your husband is a fool in all aspects where you are concerned."

Sara turned her head to the side. "Please do not refer to me in those terms."

Ian narrowed his gaze. "My love?"

Sara's lips quivered. "Please."

Sara's reaction to his endearment stunned Ian into silence. Did she not realize how madly in love with her he was? Had his every action not shown his devotion? He closed his eyes once he realized her lonely past and his insensitive actions collided. He was more of a fool than he fathomed. Sara had only ever known the love of her grandmother. Not of a gentleman who would move heaven and earth just to have her smile bestowed upon him. She didn't even realize how her friends loved her like she was their sister. Everyone Sara had ever known had failed her.

He fell to his knees in front of her and gently drew her face toward him, cupping her cheeks. "I cannot call you anything else because it would pale compared to how I care about you. You are the sweet sunshine of my days and the tempting moon of my nights. Your smile sets my heart aglow with the most amazing stars shooting from your eyes at how you approach life with a sense of bravery I admire. I love you from the very depth of my soul."

"'Tis impossible," Sara whispered.

Ian's smile widened at Sara's denial. "How so?"

"You are a duke."

"And you are my duchess."

"Only because of your sense of honor."

Ian rubbed his thumbs across Sara's cheeks. "My only sense of honor was to make you my wife before I dishonored you as my governess."

Sara blushed a fiery red. "Lust is closely misconstrued as love, Your Grace."

Ian threw his head back and roared with laughter at every deniable excuse Sara extended to describe the depth of his feelings for her. It would appear his wife needed more convincing to understand how much he loved her. With one swift movement, he rose and swept Sara into his arms, settling her on his lap. He would spend the entire day convincing her if he so needed.

"Your Grace," Sara gasped with astonishment. That only earned her a tender kiss. Ian coaxed her lips apart with the gentle pressure of his tongue. She sighed against his lips. "Ian."

"Mmm, much better," Ian murmured. Before their kiss turned into a passionate declaration of their desire for one another, he pulled back. He needed Sara to see that the connection that bound them together ran much deeper than their passion for one another.

Sara's eyes fluttered open when Ian pulled away. She almost stated how true her statement was from their kiss, but Ian's expression stopped her from uttering a single word. He stared at her with what could only be called love. It was how her friends' husbands stared at them. While passion flared behind the love, it was the love she'd been blind to. Because it was the same expression Sara had caught Ian staring at her with since they married.

She lifted her hand to trail her fingers against his temple. "You love me."

Ian captured her hand under his. "Aye."

She couldn't hold back her tears even if she tried. Dreams she'd never thought possible were within her reach if she allowed herself to be free from her past. A past filled with a loss of worthiness. Lying in Ian's arms, she finally found the love she had always craved. He loved her not because she was an obligation but because he chose to love her. She would always hold a special love for her grandmother, but Sara had noticed in rare moments that she was also a burden. One out of obligation to protect her. While Ian held the same belief, it was because of how deeply he loved her.

"I love you too," Sara confessed.

Ian moved their hands to cover his heart. "Aye, love. I have felt it here, blooming to life since the day I met you."

Sara pressed her lips against his. "I thought I had kept my feelings hidden."

"Ah, love, your eyes are the vision of your soul. Even if I couldn't see the love shining from them, your every action speaks of your love and devotion for me."

"I only want to make you proud."

He brushed his thumb across her lips. "I am honored to be your husband. You must understand I hold no one's opinion to matter but yours and yours alone."

Sara allowed Ian's confession of love to wash away any doubts she held about belonging in his life. He wasn't a gentleman to allow others to change his mind, nor would he allow them to influence the decisions he made. He was a formable duke who others sought to impress and follow. His declaration of love filled her heart with the promise of a loving future with her by his side. Whoever didn't support their marriage, Ian would never allow their opinion to stop him from loving her.

Ian relaxed back on the cushions, pulling Sara with him. He held her for a while in comfortable silence while they both absorbed the depth of their love for one another. The weight of the secrets Ian had kept from her lifted to be replaced with the reassurance of their confessions. No longer would he have to deny what he longed to share with her. While the duties of a duke and duchess would consume their lives, Ian promised to create memories where only the two of them existed.

"Where do we go from here?" Sara's question broke through their peaceful moment.

Ian caressed her arm. “I refuse to place you in harm with what we should do. I wish for us to return to Scotland with the hope that the culprit ceases his games once he realizes we are not a threat to his existence. With the help of your friends and their influence, we can secretly spread word of the investigation having ended. I believe our enquiry has only instigated the taunts, and our presence in London intensifies the danger.”

Sara turned in his arms. “Have there been more letters since our wedding?”

Ian winced. “Yes.”

Sara gave him a tight nod. “Can I read them?”

“Yes, even though I wish to shield you from them. I never meant for there to be secrets between us. You must understand, I wished to protect you from the evilness of this world.”

“I am not so fragile that I cannot handle the hardship before us.”

Ian smiled softly at her. “I know that now. However, I will always do everything in my power to prevent harm to you.”

Sara threaded her fingers through his hair to lower his head to hers. Their kiss held the promise of their future with each gentle nip of their lips as they explored the power of the words spoken between them.

“You cannot always protect me, Ian. There will be moments where I will suffer from heartache or fear, but I shall always turn to you for comfort.”

Deep in his soul, he understood what Sara meant, but he would do everything in his power so she would never have to suffer again. “Promise me you will share your doubts and fears with me and not suffer in silence any longer.”

“I promise to share the same honesty that you will share with me. Also, we will not return to Scotland. I will not give whoever taunts me the power to send us scurrying away. We will stay in London until we discover this villain. He has held his reign of power for far too long. Even if he is my father, he will not destroy us,” Sara declared.

Ian brushed a kiss on her neck. “Your bravery is an aphrodisiac to the desire I hold for you.”

Sara playfully slapped his arm. "Focus, *Your Grace*. This is what I meant about your lust."

Ian drew Sara underneath him. "What courses through my veins is far from lust, *Your Grace.* You consume my soul with a fire that burns the fiercest of flames."

"Oh" was all Sara could mutter before Ian ravished her lips with the passion burning from his soul.

She melted into him with one devouring kiss after another. She wrapped her arms around his neck, sinking her fingers into his hair. Their tongues tangled in a dance of seduction that left them breathless with an undying need. Sara had been on the verge of tugging at his cravat when a discreet cough and a knock on the door interrupted them.

"Your Grace, your guests have arrived. I have placed them in the parlor," Simmons spoke from behind the door.

"Thank you, Simmons. The duchess and I will be along soon. Please serve our guests tea while they wait," Ian ordered. He leaned his forehead against Sara's with a charming smile. "I love you, my dear."

Sara returned his smile with the sweetness he adored. "I love you, Ian. With all my heart and soul."

"A love I will treasure for an eternity." He rose and held out his hand. "Shall we join our friends?"

Sara hesitated. "They are not upset with me?"

"No, my love. They are anxious to see you are safe. Your disappearance frightened them yesterday, and they are distraught from betraying you. I believe they wish to make amends."

Sara laid her hand on his. "'Tis I who needs to make amends."

Ian led Sara from the library to the parlor. While everyone had kept Sara in the dark to protect her, she had kept her own secrets from them. She hadn't understood how her disappearance had affected her husband until he made passionate love to her with a desperation that confused her. She could only imagine her friend's despair. Ian's confession of love made her realize that she no longer needed to carry the burden of her loneliness.

She welcomed the comfort of love.

Chapter Fourteen

False Rumors

As soon as Sara stepped into the parlor, her friends surrounded her and wrapped her in their warm embrace. As they wiped the tears from their eyes, they muttered their apologies. Each lady pleaded for forgiveness, while Sara offered her own before they pulled apart. Once they separated, Ian wrapped his arm around her waist and pulled her closer. She rested her head on his arm as she smiled at her friends.

"You are well?" Vivian asked.

Sara met Ian's gaze. "Yes."

Lost in the love flowing from Ian's eyes, Sara almost forgot they were no longer alone. A few amused chuckles from across the room shook Sara from Ian's hypnotic trance. She didn't need a mirror to know her face was aflame from the warmth spreading throughout her.

Flora hooked her arm through Sara's and led her to the settee. "Aye, I can see you are well indeed. Do you not agree, Grace?"

"Indeed," Grace teased while sliding into a chair.

Vivian slid next to Sara and took pity on her. "Ladies, behave."

Ian strode across the parlor. "Gentlemen, would you care to join me for a stronger beverage?"

Ian directed the gentlemen to the corner, where he poured them each a tumbler of whiskey. They stayed away, so the ladies could visit with a modicum of privacy. While they needed to share their plans for remaining in London, he knew Sara would wish to mend her disagreement with the ladies without an audience.

"I see Sara has returned with no harm," Courtland commented.

Ian kept his gaze focused on Sara. "Yes."

"Did she ever explain where she went?" Lockhart asked.

Ian shook his head.

Hepburn patted him on the shoulder. "The only important matter is the lass is safe."

If only she were, Ian wanted to mutter. However, he kept his fear to himself. Sara would never remain safe until they revealed the culprit behind the threats. But he didn't need to voice his worry. The other gentlemen understood very well the need of ensuring their wives' safety. Sara's determination to remain in London left him powerless to prevent the villain from terrorizing her.

But not powerless to protect her.

False Rumors

Sara tried to focus on her friends, but her gaze kept straying toward Ian. He stared at her with a secret message only she understood. Who knew confessing their love for one another held such intensity? It was as if they shared the same thoughts. Did Ian wish for them to rush through their friends' visit so they could continue their intimate encounter?

"Then an elephant stampeded through Hyde Park, picking up children with his trunk and setting them on his back. The crowd grew horrified, to say the least," Flora said.

Elephant? Children? Hyde Park? Sara shook herself from her daydream. "What happened in Hyde Park?"

Grace's sparkling laughter echoed around them. "Now we have her attention."

Flora's lips twisted to the side in a teasing nature. "But for how long?"

Vivian poured the tea and attempted to redirect their conversation. "We wish to apologize for our role of keeping your husband's secrets."

"'Tis I who must apologize for my reaction. The fault lies with Ian and me for not communicating with one another on what we expect from our marriage."

"Have you now?" Vivian inquired.

Sara blushed. "Yes, we have."

Flora wrapped her arm around Sara's shoulders and squeezed. "Excellent."

"Has he confessed his love?" Grace whispered.

A secretive smile graced Sara's face, and she lost herself in Ian's stare. "Mmm."

Her friends sighed at her newfound happiness. She tore her gaze away from Ian to see their joy at her finding love too. Not only Ian's love but theirs too. She was the luckiest girl ever.

"Thank you for being the best friends a girl has."

Flora lifted her teacup. "Hear! Hear!"

They all laughed at Flora's exclamation. No other words needed to be said between them. The bond of their friendship had flourished since they met and would continue to do so. Meeting these ladies at her loneliest filled Sara's heart with much joy. Even though they had endured heartache and tribulations, their friendship had remained strong.

Soon, the gentlemen joined them to discuss their next step in luring the villain into their trap. Sara refused to disappear to Scotland without taking a stance that she deserved to marry a duke. Until the culprit received their message and they confronted him, there would be no peace in their lives.

"We do not mean to pry, but where did you disappear to yesterday?" Vivian asked.

Sara rested the teacup on the table. "A bookstore I visited when we used to live in London. The Hardys were kind enough to allow me to stay with them when I lost my position with the Baldridges. I wanted to escape where no prying eyes watched my every move and waited for me to fail."

Ian rested his hand on Sara's shoulder in a comforting gesture to show his support. Sara angled her head to brush her lips across his knuckles in appreciation. The relief of sharing her insecurities with him had lightened her heavy heart. Also, confessing her secrets to her friends without judgment allowed her the freedom to be herself.

"Did you have contact with anyone other than the Hardys?" Courtland inquired.

Sara nodded. "Lord Roselli was visiting the bookstore, and he escorted me to my carriage."

"Lord Roselli?" Ian inquired.

"Marian's friend, Lady Roselli's husband," Sara explained.

"Anyone else?" Lockhart asked.

"No," Sara answered. "Why do you ask?"

Ian pressed a kiss against her cheek before striding across the parlor to retrieve the letters for Sara. "Because I received a letter yesterday before you returned home stating how you conversed with the villain."

Sara's complexion paled as she read the letter. "Do you believe Lord Roselli is the villain behind the letters?"

"No one is innocent at this point," Hepburn declared.

Flora reached out to squeeze Sara's hand. "Have you had any other contact with Lord Roselli?"

"At the Darlington Ball before Ian surprised me with your visit."

Ian shared a secret glance with the other gentleman at what Sara's confession revealed. The connection felt significant, not coincidental. Had they unraveled the mystery that had plagued them for the past year?

The gentlemen shared a look between them, and Sara understood what she implied. An eerie sensation crawled along her spine, causing her to shake with the horror of how she had interacted with the villain himself. Not only the villain but possibly her father.

"Is Lord Roselli my father? And also the man who terrorized us this past year?"

Grace gasped. "Your father? I thought you were an orphan."

Sara clasped her hands in her lap to control their shaking. The enormity of the pieces connecting overwhelmed her. "Ian has discovered a connection between the letters and my family's secrets."

Knowing the person who tormented them shook Sara to her core. Also, understanding their connection to one another brought back memories of her youth, of wondering who her parents were. Her grandmother would never speak about them, which left Sara feeling insecure and unworthy. Now to confront how her abandonment was about her father's status in society only furthered her harsh opinion about the aristocracy.

Ian rushed over to Sara at her distress and pulled her into his arms as he explained what he'd discovered. "Through my investigation, I learned Sara's father's initials and the reason for Sara's abandonment. It is my belief that her father attempts to frighten Sara away before anyone discovers she is his child. Those implications would ruin him once everyone learns the truth."

Courtland strode to close the door. "How do you plan to use this information to draw the villain out?"

"Sara wants to remain in London. However, it would be in our family's best interest if we were to return to Scotland. Perhaps if we stay at my estate in the Highlands for a few months, it will send a message that we will keep his secret if he stops his vengeance."

"No," Sara said with firm determination. "I will not allow us to close ourselves off because of his sadistic games. He will not be the victor with his terror. We must show him a united front and destroy him as he has set to destroy us."

"Sara, it is not worth it. You do not know what evil he is capable of in his attempt to destroy you," Ian attempted to reason with her.

Sara cupped Ian's cheek. "As long as you remain by my side, he can never destroy me."

"Forever," Ian murmured before brushing a kiss across Sara's lips.

"Then we shall develop a plan to ruin this bastard once and for all," Hepburn swore.

Ian and Sara gazed into each other's eyes with a rush of emotions consuming them. Their love shined brightly with a determination to destroy their tormentor so they could pursue their happily ever after in each other's arms for an eternity.

No matter what obstacles they endured, they would do so together.

Chapter Fifteen

False Rumors

SARA FOUND HERSELF UNABLE to relax at the soothing melody of the musical. The comfort of her friends surrounding her didn't bring her joy. The suspense of the unknown kept her waiting on guard for danger to strike. They'd spent the past month accepting countless invitations to welcome her into society and attending one event after another. However, the villain had grown quiet again.

Their every attempt at drawing the culprit out to reveal himself ended without success. Ian encouraged her to remain patient, but Sara became more frustrated at the tedious progress. She had thought of the perfect enticement to lure the culprit out. However, everyone had agreed the danger wasn't worth her safety. They feared her idea might provoke the villain into harming her. But Sara disagreed.

During intermission, she would put her plan into action. It was best she didn't inform Ian or her friends of her intentions. For them to act in surprise and for their reaction to be authentic, she must catch them unaware. She only hoped they saw through her performance and played alongside her. If not, her plan would fail, and their lives would remain stagnant with uncertainty.

Her eyes drifted closed to calm her nerves by absorbing the beauty of the notes playing in perfect harmony. She detested deceit of any form. However, she must present herself to the ton as they viewed her. A person below her station who had tricked the duke into marrying her to rise in society with wealth and power at her disposal. An image far from the truth but one that would strike the villain's retaliation.

As the song ended, everyone rose from their seats to mingle with the other guests. Ian slid her hand into the crook of his arm as he guided them near the windows. He preferred them to stand where no one caught them unaware and he could view the room at large. With his status as a duke, he didn't need to socialize unless he preferred to. His stance remained strong. He would snub those who wouldn't accept Sara as his wife. It was their loss and his gain to have her all to himself.

They stood by themselves as their friends wandered from couple to couple. They socialized to draw out information to help them solve the mystery of who tormented them.

Ian waved a waiter over to them and handed Sara a glass of champagne. "Would you prefer something milder, my dear?"

Sara took a deep breath. "I would prefer if we could leave. This musical is a bore."

A gasp sounded from her side, and Sara kept a bored expression on her face instead of wincing at her rudeness. She had timed her response to the exact moment the hostess arrived to greet them. To add to Lady Newburn's discomfort, Sara arched her eyebrow in disdain only a duchess could do. She hoped to succeed with her crass behavior.

"Sara," Ian hissed.

Sara ignored him, tossing back the champagne in one swallow. "Waiter," she called out. "I will take another."

The waiter rushed over, and Sara replaced her empty glass with a full one she drank just as rapidly. The effect of the alcohol disagreed with her, and a round of hiccups shook her body. However, she refused to hide her distress with a demure gesture. Instead, those near them heard the disturbing sounds and stared at her in disapproval. As much as she wished to crawl away in embarrassment, she must continue with her performance until Ian forced them to leave.

Whispers spread across the room of her behavior, stirring up a round of gossip Sara hoped would reach the villain. Soon her friends circled them to keep the peering gazes of the ton from seeing her, which was the opposite of what Sara needed to achieve success with her plan.

She grabbed another glass. "I would love to make a toast to my amazing friends," Sara slurred.

Ian removed the glass from her hand and passed it to Vivian. "I fear you have overindulged this evening, my love."

Sara attempted to claim the glass again, only to bump into Grace and Flora. "Nonsense. I am only celebrating being your duchess. A feat I thought I would never achieve." She threw her arms in the air and raised her voice. "But I persevered and won the title." She lowered her voice to a loud whisper. "And all that it entails."

Vivian shot Ian a look filled with sympathy before wrapping her arm around Sara's shoulder. "Perhaps some fresh air will do Sara good. Flora and Grace, will you please join Sara and me for a spell?"

Vivian didn't wait to see if Flora and Grace followed as she ushered Sara out the French doors onto the terrace. However, there was more to Sara's act. Her performance thus far hadn't held the desired effect.

"Can you believe the atrocious dress Lady Newburn wore to host this musical? So drab and unbecoming. I must give her the name of my modiste. But then I suppose she cannot afford the dresses Somerville has gifted me. Along with the other ladies in attendance, no doubt. They cannot dress so grand either. Not to mention wear the quality of jewels I am able to." Sara ran her fingers across the jewels of her necklace. "Why, this necklace alone is more than everyone's yearly income."

"Please refrain yourself," Vivian reprimanded.

Sara jerked out of Vivian's grasp and flounced across the terrace to slide across a bench hidden between some greenery. Darkness might've shrouded them, but Sara made out the disapproving glare from Vivian and Grace. However, she hadn't fooled Flora for even a second, because her friend fought to keep her laughter at bay, but she failed once Sara threw her arm across her eyes in the dramatic pose of a pretentious duchess. Flora's laughter floated around them, coaxing Sara to dissolve into giggles. If she could fool Vivian and Grace, then the other guests were fooled by her fall from grace. Sara didn't regret one second of her act, even if she struck Ian's ire.

Grace's mouth opened and closed at Sara's behavior, but she was unable to utter a rebuke worthy of her performance. Vivian's eyes narrowed when she realized what Sara had done to ruin her reputation. However, her disappointment soon turned into pride at how Sara had jumped off a ledge to regain her life.

Flora clapped. "What an amazing performance."

Grace swung her head to stare at Flora in astonishment. "Are you mad? She has ruined any chance of society accepting her."

Flora waved her hand in the air. "A blessing in disguise, I must say."

Grace growled. "Sara has created a scandal she will never recover from."

"I do not believe she cares about her status in society as much as she wishes for the normalcy she most desires with Somerville," Vivian murmured.

"It was an act."

Sara nodded at Grace's statement.

Grace joined Sara on the bench. "Are you not worried about how they might perceive you?"

"No. I only care about how my friends feel about me and Ian's love and support."

"Which you have, no matter how vexing your actions may be," Ian growled from behind them.

Sara sat ramrod straight with her hands in her lap and her chin jutted out at Ian's tone. While he stated his support, Sara recognized the disappointment in his voice. However, the desire blazing from his gaze spoke of something more sinister than he had ever expressed before. Had she pressed her luck with her performance? Would Ian send her away to keep his standing in society as pristine as it had been before he married her?

Hepburn whistled. "Who knew the timid governess possessed such a backbone?"

Ian kept his intense gaze focused on Sara. "I did."

Still, Sara never wavered. To convince Ian and their friends of her bravery, she couldn't falter before their very eyes. "I had no other choice."

"While this evening's performance might tarnish your reputations, Sara is correct," Courtland stated.

"Aye," Lockhart agreed. "Our plan has not worked to our advantage of late."

"The question remains if Sara's actions will provoke the villain to act with his usual form of vengeance," Vivian stated.

"If so, with the safeguards we put into place, 'tis only a matter of time before we catch the bastard and end this madness once and for all." Ian held out his hand to Sara. "In the meantime, 'tis best if my wife and I make our departure before Lord Newburn makes the grave error of ordering a duke and duchess from his home."

Hepburn wrapped his arm around Flora's waist. "Aye. We will rejoin the masses and continue Sara's performance with our own mix of distaste for her actions."

Grace brushed Sara's cheek with a kiss. "Forgive us, dear, but we must show our revulsion for your behavior."

Sara nodded. "There is nothing to forgive. A necessity if it helps to end the terror that has consumed our lives for the past year."

Silence descended on them as their friends made their way back inside. Sara peeked a glance at Ian to see him staring through the windows with a frown. His distance swirled the emotions in her gut into a whirlwind of doubt. She couldn't tell if he was furious with her behavior or if he supported her decision. The longer he took to react, the more uneasy Sara felt. When his gaze narrowed and his grip tightened, Sara understood without a doubt that she had disappointed him. She had shamed him in front of his peers and proved them correct that he was foolish to marry a nobody below their station. Even though she did so to protect them, the result of her actions proved otherwise.

Sara closed her eyes and lowered her head. "Forgive me, Ian," she whispered.

Ian walked them toward the entrance and snarled. "Hold your head high, *Duchess,* if you want to convince them of your pomposity."

Sara stiffened at the edge of his tone and the steely gaze he penetrated her with. No matter his reaction, she couldn't waver in her stance without admitting defeat. Their audience expected her to walk past them with her head held down in shame from Ian's reprimand. However, she pasted on the look of superiority and sauntered through the crowd with an expectation of them bowing at her feet because she had graced them with her presence.

The hissing of whispers echoed around them as they left the musical. Not once did she falter with her performance. Sara had had a goal when she set out to act with such obnoxious behavior and she would depart satisfied that she had achieved success with her performance. She would face Ian's wrath with the grace of her true character once they were alone.

They sat across from one another in silence during the carriage ride. Sara was wise enough to wait for Ian to address her. Each maddening second passed quietly, only intensifying her anxiousness. It wasn't until they left the trail of other carriages behind that he crooked his finger for her to come to him. However, he never moved an inch to make room for her on the cushions, which left her to kneel at his feet in between his spread legs.

Ian didn't give Sara a chance to react to his demand before he bent over and speared his hands through her hair, sending her hairpins clanking to the carriage floor. He ravished her lips with the desperation of a man in fear for his lady. He had never been prouder of Sara, taking control of their nerve-racking predicament with her brave performance. Yet, her bravery left him in fear for her life. Her actions placed a target on her. He worried he couldn't protect her from the consequences of her actions.

His tongue forced her lips apart so he could savor the sweetness Sara exuded with every breath she took. Their tongues tangled in a passionate exchange with the ferocity of their fraught emotions. Their lips melded together as he consumed Sara's sighs with his growls of pleasure. The unknown before them left Ian desperate to claim Sara. He needed to feel her heart pressed against his, beating as one. She would only remain safe while in his arms.

He tore at the buttons on her cloak and swept it away from her shoulders in one tug. The buttons on the back of her dress, however, didn't receive the same treatment as he ripped at the dress in one resounding tear that caused Sara to pull away from their kiss. Her ragged, indrawn breath should've been the tipping point for him to cease his desperate attempt to claim her. However, the sight before him only intensified the need coursing through him.

Sara knelt on her knees before him with her hair flowing around her in a tousled mess from his touch, with her breasts heaving from their passionate kiss. The moonlight cast a glow on her pearly skin that left him aching to caress her globes and draw her sweet cherries between his lips while she rode his cock to completion. When she struck her tongue across her lips, plump from their kisses, he lost what control he barely clung to.

"Undo my trousers," Ian ordered.

Sara didn't hesitate to do Ian's bidding. The grave tone of his order swept through Sara like a tidal wave of shameless desire she needed to satisfy. Ian's behavior pushed the edge of a passion she longed to explore with him. The mixed emotions swirling in his gaze left her with no room to refuse him, even if she wanted to. However, she held no desire to.

She slid her palms along the inside of his thighs and undid his trousers with trembling fingers. He had never requested her to perform to his needs in their intimate encounters. However, his intention of what he wanted from her was clear with how he leaned back against the cushions and watched her with his eyelids lowered. He waited with patience for her to proceed without his instruction.

Her inexperience would've caused her to hesitate before this evening. However, still heady with the power she'd wielded at the musical, it gave her the confidence to seduce her husband. Her body. But most of all, her love. She would tempt Ian with one loving touch after another.

Ian thought he had control over their intimacy with his order, but the flare of Sara's siren gaze should've been a warning to his confidence. However, she fooled him with how her fingers trembled as she swept his cock into her hand like a seasoned mistress. But when her fingers closed around his cock and glided up and down, he realized he was at the mercy of her pleasure. He hissed when she bent her head to lick the juices from the tip.

Sara raised her head at his hiss, unsure if she had done something wrong. He closed his eyes for a brief second to control himself from spending in her hand before he had the pleasure of enjoying her lips wrapped around him while she brought him to the pinnacle of satisfaction. His eyes flashed open when Sara wrapped her lips around the head and sucked softly before drawing his cock deep into her mouth.

"Holy hell," Ian gasped.

His wife might be an innocent in the art of sucking his cock, but her eagerness to please him only amplified the desire consuming him. He tried to control himself, but his hips arched off the seat as he pressed deeper inside her sweet-as-sin mouth. Her tongue only added to his destruction with each slide as he set a rhythm for her to follow. His hands tangled in her hair again with a firm grip in his search to find fulfillment.

However, Sara was relentless in her seduction with each delicious lick of her tongue against his cock. She left him hanging onto the edge near the flames as she teased him by pulling her mouth away to flick her tongue against the slit to savor his juices. To closing her mouth around him again and swallowing deeply.

When her touch gentled with whisper-soft kisses along the length of his cock, he went mad with a need to sink deeply into the warmth of her pussy and claim her as he had never before. With urgency, he pulled her up to straddle his lap and plunged into her with a thrust that left them both breathless. Her wetness welcomed him as if it had waited an eternity for the connection between them.

Sara's dress draped off her shoulders in a tattered mess, teasing him with glimpses of her breasts. He finished his destruction and tore it from her arms, along with her chemise. Her nipples hardened under his stare, begging for him to claim them. He licked his lips before lowering his head and drawing one into his mouth. He wasn't gentle but sucked the bud hard until Sara writhed on his lap with a need she had yet to voice to his satisfaction. Only whimpers spilled from her lips. But he was a greedy bastard who wanted her to beg for her release.

His lips trailed a path of fire to her other breast, where he teased her nipple with the flick of his tongue before taking a soft bite at the sweetness. Her hips arched against him in a silent request for him to move. How he found the power to remain still was beyond him. Perhaps he didn't want to find gratification so soon after the torment she put him through with her rash behavior. Or else it was how alive he felt with her pussy gripping his throbbing cock, with their passion swirling around them, demanding release.

Sara had gone past the moment of madness when Ian took her by surprise by pulling her onto his lap and entering her with an intensity that left her shaking with a need she found impossible to describe. His attention to her breasts only intensified the desire exploding through her. Still, he teased her by staying still and not moving with the sway of her hips against his. When she pressed down against him, his hand tightened around her breast, sending shockwaves straight to her core, alighting every nerve on alert for his touch.

"Ian."

Her breathy moan shifted Ian's attention from her breasts to sliding his hand under her skirts to press his thumb against her clit with teasing flicks. His tongue teased its own magic along the length of her neck to under her ear. Sara could take the madness no more and yanked on his hair for him to meet her lips. His soft chuckle only fueled the passion urging her to take satisfying their needs into her own hands.

She rose up and rotated her hips with the tip of his cock, teasing her pussy, then she lowered herself with slow precision before grinding on his lap. Her actions led to Ian grabbing her hips and pressing upward. Sara threw her head back at the exquisite sensation of his cock sliding in and out of her while Ian lost control.

He had underestimated his wife and the control she yielded over him with her innocent reactions to the pleasures he sought from her mind, body, and soul. While he teased her until she begged, she struck out to seek her own pleasures from him. His wife was an innocent temptress he craved every second of every day. Every encounter elicited an enlightening connection nothing could ever sever. Sara enraptured his attention with every look, kiss, and caress.

"Wrap your arms around me, love," Ian encouraged.

Sara followed Ian's directions like the demure governess he had fallen in love with. However, ever since their bodies had joined as one, he knew her to be anything but demure. She was a fiery goddess. He would spend an eternity bowing at her feet with his love and devotion. She held his gaze while her fingers tangled in his hair. Their bodies moved as one with each slide of his cock claiming her pussy as his.

Sara lost herself in Ian's gaze. The love shining from his eyes gave her the courage to be the soul she'd always wanted to be. He allowed her to be the fierce lady by his side, keeping the honest qualities she valued about herself, all the while showing her he would stand by her side at all costs. She clung to him as he heightened their pleasure with stroke after stroke in and out of her.

Sara pressed her lips against his in the softest of kisses as pleasure overtook them.

Ian pulled Sara closer, never wanting to release her. As they succumbed to the ecstasy of their passion, the force of his love for Sara overwhelmed him to where he allowed his greatest fears to paralyze him. If he ever lost Sara, he'd be incapable of survival. The love he held for her far surpassed any love he had ever felt for anyone else.

Sara lifted her head from Ian's shoulder and laid her hand on his cheek. "I love you, Ian."

He gripped her hand. "Not nearly as much as I love you, my dear Sara."

Her husband was a paradox of a gentleman on this carriage ride home. From a disgruntled duke to a passionate lover to a loving husband. Every single one she loved more than she could express. There were no grand words to define how she felt about Ian. Only the three simple words she spoke showed the depth of her emotions for this sweet man. Her behavior this evening showed everyone she didn't deserve the duke's love. However, what she shared with Ian in privacy was all that mattered.

Or so she hoped.

Chapter Sixteen

False Rumors

Ian carried Sara abovestairs to their chamber. Wrapped in his coat, Sara could feel the blush washing over her about how she would explain the tattered ruins of her dress. While Ian could behave any way he pleased, there would be talk of her scandalous behavior amongst the servants. And gossip never remained inside a household. It would soon spread to other households, and would play in her favor, considering she'd caused room for the gossipmongers to have free rein with her character.

Ian set her near the bed and helped her out of her dress. He kissed her shoulder. "I owe you a new dress."

Sara turned in his arms. "Nay. I have too many as it is."

He eased her chemise off. "You can never have too many."

Sara tugged on his cravat and slid the buttons undone on his vest and shirt. "After this evening, you are to banish me to your estate, not spoil me with new dresses."

Ian slid his arms around Sara and trailed his hand up the smooth expanse of her back. "I would love to banish you to my estate and have my wicked way with you."

Sara frowned playfully at him. "That is not what I meant. My banishment is my punishment for my behavior this evening."

Ian nipped her lips. "Why should I punish you when I could not be prouder of you?"

She feathered her fingers through his hair. "You are not furious with my acting out?"

He stepped back and finished disrobing before sliding them into bed. "Not so much furious, but I worry for your safety at your bold attempt to draw out the villain."

She rolled over to lie across his chest. "Do you not mean Lord Roselli, my father?"

"We are not positive your father and the villain are the same."

While they held no proof of the connection, the clues proved they might be correct. However, Lord and Lady Roselli had made themselves scarce from the social scene the past few weeks. Along with the villain's silence, it proved too much of a coincidence for them to be anything different.

Sara cocked her eyebrow. "Are we not?"

Ian rolled them over. "Do you remember the pact we made to no longer keep secrets?"

Sara grimaced at how she'd betrayed Ian with her actions. "I apologize for my deceit. However, I had to keep you in the dark to make it authentic for everyone to believe."

"I understand your aim, and I am astounded by your bravery. But for your safety, will you promise no more surprises until this has ended?"

Sara twined her arms around Ian's neck. "I promise no more surprises."

And she meant it. This evening was their last attempt to strike the villain's wrath. If she didn't succeed, then she feared nothing would ever end their torment unless they escaped far from society. Something she had no intention of doing. She refused to live in fear for the rest of her life. However, if needed, she would sacrifice her happiness for Ian and Mairi.

Sara prayed she never had to.

False Rumors

Sara watched Mairi skip around the garden path. While they wanted to visit the park with their friends, they stayed close to home for Ian to watch over them. The threat of the unknown had escalated since the spectacle she'd made at the Newburn Musical a few days ago. Gossip had spread about her scandalous behavior, and in so, the ton had labeled her a pariah nobody wanted to socialize with.

To keep up appearances, her friends' company remained elusive. While it was all an act, their absence affected Sara to a profound degree. She longed to share her fears with them. However, they must stay away for the villain to believe he'd succeeded in his vengeance by ostracizing her. He thought he was the victor with his revenge. Except Sara had never felt more content than with a quiet lifestyle surrounded by her loved ones.

She had never loved another soul more than she loved Ian. Ever since they confessed their love, he'd sought her throughout the day to spend time with her and Mairi. Not to mention the moments he stole kisses when he thought no one watched. Or when he coerced her to partake in intimate acts of lovemaking throughout the townhome. Everyone thought her husband was a prim and proper duke, but he was the most scandalous of gentlemen, one she found much bliss with.

Mairi skipped to Sara. "Momma, when can we visit our friends at the park?"

Sara wrapped Mairi's scarf around her neck. "Soon, love."

"Can we invite them to our home?"

Sara sighed about how to explain the delicate subject to a child without causing confusion and fear. Until now, Mairi had never questioned why they kept to the townhome, instead of exploring London as they had when they first arrived. They had pacified her by showering Mairi with their attention. However, she was a child who longed for children her own age to interact with. It was cruel of them to keep her isolated but necessary to keep her protected. Sara wished this madness would end soon.

She cringed at the lie she must tell Mairi. "Your friends have been busy with their own families. But I promise soon, we shall invite them over."

"All right. Can we go inside for some hot chocolate?"

Sara tapped Mairi on the nose. "We sure can."

The beauty of innocent children was their acceptance to believe adults only ever told the truth. Guilt settled in Sara's gut at how she had to lie to her daughter, even though it was for her protection. If Sara hadn't accepted Ian's proposal, then Mairi would be free to explore the possibilities before her without restrictions.

They held hands as they walked inside. Sara helped Mairi off with her coat and handed the coats to a maid. Another maid took Mairi to the kitchen for her hot chocolate and a treat. Sara promised to join her for a story after she talked to Ian. She needed to convince him to take Mairi out for an afternoon excursion to lighten her visit to London. If not, then Sara worried Mairi would become withdrawn again. The predicament they found themselves in wasn't Mairi's fault, and she shouldn't have to suffer another minute longer.

"Do you know where I might find the duke?" Sara asked a footman.

"He is in the parlor with Lord and Lady Whetham."

Sara nodded. "Thank you."

Sara almost strolled into the parlor to discuss her concerns with Ian and the Whethams but paused outside the doorway when her name was mentioned. Eavesdropping was disgraceful, but Ian's fervent response as he refused to agree with the Whethams kept her back.

"I refuse to place Sara in a setting that will cause her harm. Not to mention the cruelty toward her if she attended," Ian growled.

"Your refusal is nonsense. You have been waiting for this invitation. You cannot isolate the poor girl in an act of protection," Lord Whetham argued.

"We will remain by her side the entire visit," Lady Whetham pleaded.

Sara peeked around the door to see Ian pacing across the rug, dragging his hand through his hair. She wished to relieve his agitation but couldn't until she learned what they discussed. To do so, she must interrupt them. However, she held back to hear more. She feared if she walked inside, Ian would cover their discussion with another topic to hide his worries.

"If you do not accept the invitation, then you risk losing the girl," Lord Whetham warned.

Ian paused. "Is that a threat?"

Lady Whetham rose and urged Ian to sit. She shot a warning look at her husband to cease his ramblings. "No, 'tis no threat. Just a warning for you to understand how this ordeal has impacted Sara. Her behavior has caused her to act out by such drastic measures."

Sara bit back a gasp. Nothing good ever came out of listening to others' conversations, no matter how one twisted their reasons. While the Whethams had shown Sara support for her outburst at the musical, it was only a farce to protect her feelings. She'd never wanted to embarrass this family, but her every action brought forth shame to their good name. Perhaps it was for the best if she made herself scarce. After a while, Ian could resume the life he was born into, one not ruined by marrying his governess. He would weather the scandal with his distinguished persona and hopefully find the happiness he deserved.

The villain's primary agenda this past year had been to scare Sara away from the aristocracy. With her gone, Ian and her friends could live their lives without discord. She had been the target all along, and she must admit defeat before she hurt those she loved even more. Her heartache paled in comparison to the torment she placed upon them if she remained.

With newfound determination, Sara stepped back and hurried to their suite. She must disappear with haste. Soon Mairi would finish her treat and seek her out to read a story before her nap. Not to mention, Ian would find her to assure himself that she remained safe.

Sara rushed to pull the beautiful day dress from her body and redressed in a dull day dress she'd worn as Ian's governess. She had kept her belongings in a valise tucked away in her wardrobe because of her insecure thoughts that Ian had suffered from madness when he asked her to be his bride. He had proven his sanity by wrapping her in a cocoon of ever-binding love and doting on her every day. She would treasure those memories for a lifetime spent alone so they could live a peaceful life without the drama of her remaining in their lives.

She sat on the bed to tug on her walking boots when she noticed the letter on her pillowcase. Her heart lurched at the sight, and tears slid along her cheeks. Ian had taken to writing her tokens of his affections every day, leaving the notes in random places for her to find. Some were as simple as him telling her he loved her, while he filled the other letters with poems that compared his love affair with her. It was the last letter she would ever receive from him.

She trailed her fingers along the parchment, deciding if her bravery extended to reading his latest confession of love or if she should leave it behind to save herself the agony. However, there was no question about what she desired. His declaration would comfort her during the lonely days ahead. She tore open the letter in her anxious rush to read his loving words before she left his life forever.

Desperate for the reassurance of Ian's adoration, Sara turned numb at the threat leaping off the parchment. There were no words to describe the fear clutching her in place. She should rush to Ian with the letter so he could investigate how it had arrived, but the cruelty kept her firmly in place and only resounded her decision to leave. Nothing good would result if she remained to fight against a phantom from her past, a person she had never met but one who terrorized her because he regretted she ever existed.

My Darling Sara,

I hope you do not mind the intimacy of my greeting. For how else should I greet my daughter, my only living offspring? One I fought not to exist. However, your bitch of a mother has always been a devious soul. I should have never entangled myself with her. However, I found her attraction too difficult to resist. Even after her cunning agenda, I fell into her manipulative trap and married her. While I should feel pride about how our daughter has achieved the same lofty goal as her mother to marry above her station, I cannot. Because it would draw attention to the time of your conception, a brief moment of the past that is best to stay forgotten, for reasons it would be foolish of me to explain to you.

When your mother learned of her mother's death last year, we worried you would come searching for us. When you never did, we felt immense relief. That was, until you and your friends caused quite a scandal over your love affair with Lord Baldridge. Quite the tart like your mother, you are. Our only recourse was to prevent the ton from realizing your connection to us. So we set out to scare your friends, only for our plans to fail. Their lofty expectations only secured them protection in their marriages. So we thought to isolate you from them, but your precious duke kept ruining our plans.

You sank your claws into him so much that he made you his duchess, a position we couldn't afford you to be in. But it only shows how enamored a gentleman becomes when his whore posing as his governess spreads her thighs so readily for him. You are your mother's daughter, my dear. A slut whose only agenda is to secure herself the riches she believes she deserves. Has Somerville realized yet how devious his duchess is?

Oh, you thought you had everybody fooled by your demure governess act? Everyone thought you were naïve about life's realities. However, now they are the fools who showed you their support. Where are your friends now after you showed your true intentions at the Newburn Musical? Word is, they have deserted you, and your husband hides you away in shame. He may spout nonsense about how he keeps you away from society for your protection, but what you do not know is how he consults with his attorney daily. He attempts to dissolve his marriage to a lying cunt who infiltrated his life with her lies and deceit.

Sara gasped and clutched the letter to her chest. These had to be lies. Weren't they? She swiped at her eyes to continue, even though her heart was breaking into a million pieces.

I hope from the past few days of silence you have learned your lesson about where you belong. Far away from here. If you leave today, your mother and I will cease our terror. Your friends can live the rest of their lives in peace if you stop all contact with them. And Somerville and his darling daughter can resume their prestigious place in the hierarchy of society they were born into before they sullied their reputations by welcoming you into their lives. A lowly soul who nobody ever wanted to begin with.

If you do not leave, I cannot promise how far I will take my vengeance. Perhaps Mairi would benefit from a visit. After all, with your marriage to Somerville, I am now her grandfather. She would need my influence, considering how you will tarnish her with your misguided intentions. We would not want you to teach her how to gain a gentleman's attention. No need for her to follow in your footsteps. She must remain as pure as a white blanket of snow. Do you not agree, daughter? Something to ponder while making your decision.

Hopefully, for your sake, this will be the end of our correspondence.

Your loving father.

The letter dropped to the floor as Sara rushed to Ian's desk. She paused with indecision. She refused to write him a letter filled with deceit. But if she wrote about how she left for his best interest, he would search far and wide for her. She must disappear without a trace. She couldn't afford to leave behind any clues about where she might go.

Sara gathered her belongings, leaving behind everything Ian had ever given her, except for her wedding ring. She could never part with the gift that symbolized his love and devotion. However, she would leave behind her heart. It was the only reminder she would leave for them, because she had lost it the first day she met Ian and Mairi. She only hoped they never discarded it.

Because she would never forget their love.

Chapter Seventeen

False Rumors

"SARA ONLY CAUSED THE scene at the musical because she became desperate to end the terror ruling our lives," Ian attempted to explain Sara's actions to his in-laws.

Marian patted Ian's hand. "We understand, dear, and we do not blame Sara. We only want you to understand how this ordeal has affected Sara. Your love has blinded you from noticing the changes in her. She has withdrawn, and sadness and guilt linger in her eyes."

Stuart poured Ian a whiskey. "Only a confrontation will end this farce. Lord and Lady Roselli have given us the opportunity to do so."

Ian threw back the whiskey. "Not an opportunity. A trap."

"Perhaps," Stuart agreed. "But one we must enter to end this drama."

Ian swiped his hand across his face in frustration at how he must risk his wife's welfare to end the villain's revenge. He was uncomfortable with placing his wife in the path of danger. However, with correct precision, he could manipulate the danger to his benefit. Their friends had written to him this morning about how they had received the same invitation. He thought if he ignored the villain's summons, their terror would disappear, but his in-laws made him face the reality of the situation.

Would Sara's bravery last through this ordeal? He worried her fragile disposition might crumble from the pressure. While his wife was the bravest soul he knew, he wasn't blind to how it affected her. He witnessed it whenever he gazed upon her and stole kisses from her lips. He would do anything to see happiness shining from her eyes and her charming laughter filling his soul.

"Send our acceptance," Somerville conceded.

"We will keep her protected like the daughter she has become in our hearts," Marian promised.

Somerville nodded. Sara had impacted more than his and Mairi's life. She had given his in-laws hope for a future they had lost when Claudia passed away. Everyone's devotion to keeping her protected showed how much they loved Sara. He prayed their love would keep her sheltered in the upcoming days.

He didn't have a clue what they would walk into. From the tone of the villain's letters, it could only be a trap. However, they couldn't ignore the taunt and must face the evil invitation with a purpose Roselli would never expect. Ian swore to destroy the people whose only intention was to harm Sara.

"Poppa." Mairi ran into the parlor and jumped on Ian's lap.

Ian smiled at his daughter. "I thought you and your momma were playing in the garden."

"It was too cold. I came in for hot chocolate. But now I cannot find Momma to read me a story."

Ian raised his head in a silent question to the maid who followed Mairi into the parlor. The maid stood with her hands behind her back and paled at his attention. Something was amiss, and the girl didn't want to cause alarm with his daughter present. He picked up on the silent message and focused his attention on Marian, who must've noticed the same behavior because she rose and picked Mairi off his lap.

"How about I read you a story instead?"

Mairi wrapped her arms around her grandmother's neck. "The one about the prince who cannot find the fairy princess."

Marian's lips trembled with a smile. "Of course."

His daughter's request hit too close to the truth. Mairi, not finding Sara, caused panic to ripple through the room. Once Marian left with Mairi, Ian leapt from the chair and stalked toward the maid. He frightened her with his reaction, and he attempted to calm himself before demanding answers he feared. However, the maid understood his reaction because they had kept the servants informed of their situation. They needed them to remain vigilant about any suspicious behavior they could report.

The maid handed him a letter. "I found this near your bed when Mairi went looking for the duchess in your suite."

The maid didn't wait for his reaction and fled the parlor. Probably to inform the other servants of her discovery. He couldn't blame the lass for gossiping when it would only be for their benefit. If it helped to keep his family protected, then he would be the first to spread the news.

"What is it?" Stuart asked behind him.

Somerville didn't need to read the despicable letter to understand how his wife would've reacted to it. He thrust the letter into his father-in-law's hand and left to find Sara. However, everywhere he searched, she was nowhere to be found. When he searched the garden, he found the scarf she'd worn the day she arrived in Scotland. It rested in the place Sara had hidden before they were married. He gathered the ragged but well-cared-for garment and sank down on the bench.

She had left them.

It was her attempt to keep them protected, an act he had failed concerning Sara. He lifted the scarf to inhale the sweet scent of his wife. The love of his life. A lady he would search the ends of the earth to bring back home. He refused to allow the evil that tormented them to claim victory.

He strode back inside to send word to Courtland, Lockhart, and Hepburn of the latest development and request their aid in bringing the bastard to justice. No more niceties. He would strike with vengeance. He should've done so the second he learned the truth about Sara's tormentor's identity.

Ian scrolled out his request with urgency and handed the letters to Simmons. "Please deliver these with undue haste. Also, I need you to question the staff if they noticed any suspicious visitors before the Sara departed. I need to learn about any information that led to the duchess's disappearance."

Simmons bowed. "Yes, Your Grace. This arrived while you were in the garden."

Ian ripped the letter open to read the latest taunt. It would appear the servants hadn't been diligent in keeping the villain from entering the townhome. As with the other letters, it was a mystery he would never solve until he confronted the bastard.

Somerville,

Tsk, tsk. It seems you have lost your wife. You do not safeguard your possessions very well. Do not despair. I shall make it my mission to see to her welfare. Or will you come to her rescue as the white knight she believes you to be?

The only question remaining is if you will find her before I do.

Until then ...

Ian balled his hands into fists and stormed to the foyer. "Simmons, bring my carriage around at once," he bellowed.

"Did you find Sara?" Stuart asked.

"No. I must find her before the bastard does. If he hasn't already," Somerville growled.

"Read this." Stuart handed Somerville the letter. "He is as sadistic as we feared. I never imagined the Rosellis to be so cruel. We underestimated them all these years. 'Tis our fault for introducing Sara to them."

Somerville read through the letter and could only imagine Sara's heartache at learning her parents' intent toward her. They wished she had never existed. How those words must've tormented her. When he read the lies about him and the haunting words about Mairi, Ian went mad with his need for vengeance. However, before he struck his revenge, he needed to reassure his in-laws.

He squeezed Stuart's shoulder. "You are not at fault. They hid their deception well from everyone, including me. However, with your help and Sara's friends, we will end their reign in the ton with the disgrace they deserve."

"Whatever you need," Stuart promised.

"When Sara's friends arrive, show them this letter. The gentlemen will understand what to do. Ask the ladies to keep Marian and Mairi entertained until I can bring Sara home safely," Ian requested.

Stuart nodded. "You have my promise."

Ian strode to his carriage with demands of the driver about their first stop. He prayed Sara ran to the friends who had no connection to the aristocracy. If she wasn't there, then he had no clue where else to search. However, he refused to admit defeat. He wouldn't return home until he held Sara in his warm embrace.

The only place she needed to be.

As she fled London, Sara longed for the comfort of Ian's arms. But it was those arms she ran from. She couldn't confide in her friends or else they would convince her to return to Ian. At one time, she could have run to the Hardys' bookshop. However, Ian would search for her there after she'd admitted she ran there whenever she wanted to escape from her troubles. Her husband would turn London upside down to find her. She was a fool for leaving the letter behind. However, she had no wish to read those damaging and hurtful words ever again.

Instead, she boarded a carriage traveling to Fordwich. Sara would hide away at her grandmother's cottage until she decided how to start anew, away from everyone she loved. It was her only option for Ian and Mairi to live a drama-free life. She never imagined her marriage to Ian would become so complicated.

Since she traveled by mail carriage, she had to endure many stops along the way and the carriage's broken wheel that needed to be replaced. When she finally arrived in the village from her past, she followed the path to her grandmother's cottage. She had promised her grandmother on her deathbed to explore all that life offered. Instead, she returned to the very place she wished to avoid. The place used to hold comforting memories. Now it was a reminder of her grandmother's secrets.

With nightfall on the cusp of arriving, Sara hurried inside to light a few candles so darkness wouldn't shroud her in its midst. She would need to gather firewood to warm the cottage and gather provisions before she settled in for the evening. When she left for London for her first governess position, her grandmother's neighbor had promised to look after the cottage. When Sara stepped inside, she noticed the cottage clean and a stack of firewood near the hearth.

She fell onto the settee and took a deep breath. Mental and physical exhaustion took hold from the torment of the past year. Her emotions were a scattered mess that left her on the verge of tears more than she cared to count. She wanted to weep in Ian's arms. However, he would never have the chance at a fresh start if she returned.

Sara closed her eyes to bring herself under control. However, her lack of sleep had her drifting away. Her last thoughts were of Ian and Mairi holding their arms wide, showing her their love.

Sara never thought to question the state of the cottage. She had assumed the neighbor kept it stocked, waiting for her return. Instead, her worst nightmare had prepared for her arrival, one who watched her from the hallway in eager anticipation to strike his vengeance. Her gravest mistake was to return to the scene of the crime.

Her only hope was the husband she'd run from.

False Rumors

Somerville banged on the glass pane of the door, but to his frustration, no one answered. However, he wouldn't allow it to deter him. He would wait there until they opened the next day to see Sara unharmed inside. He continued knocking, hoping they would tire of the racket he made for their attention. It wasn't much longer when a light appeared, and a couple peered out the window.

"Please let me in." Somerville knocked again.

The man pointed at the closed sign hanging in the window. "Come back in the morning."

"I am not here to buy your damned books. I must speak with Sara," Somerville demanded.

The woman shot her husband a worried look, which caused him to unlock and open the door for Somerville. Somerville strode inside and moved to the stairs that led to their quarters, not waiting for their permission. He had never abused the power of his rank with those below him in station. But then he'd never been desperate to find his wife before. He would make his apologies once he found Sara safe.

He entered their furnishings and stumbled to a halt in the meager confines. "Where is Sara?"

"You will not find your wife here, Your Grace."

Somerville turned in confusion at the lady's sorrowful tone. "If she is not here, then where is she?"

The gentleman walked around the apartment, lighting candles. "Please take a seat, Your Grace, and my wife will try to explain where Sara might be."

Somerville had no other option than to sit at the rickety table. Mrs. Hardy bustled around the kitchen, preparing a pot of tea. He didn't have the time for such niceties, but he didn't dare ruin his chances of obtaining any information they might share about Sara's whereabouts.

"Please. I have no time to spare," Somerville pleaded.

Mrs. Hardy sat across from him. "I warned Sara not to return here after her last visit."

Somerville frowned. "Sara never mentioned such a warning. Why?"

The lady glanced at her husband, and he nodded his encouragement to tell Somerville the truth. "Because after her last visit, my husband noticed Lord Roselli lingering outside the shoppe after he helped Sara to her carriage. When he visited daily, I realized a lord of his rank would not visit our shoppe because of an interest in our catalog. His actions reflected his intention to catch Sara unaware."

"Do you know who Lord Roselli is to Sara?" Somerville asked.

"Aye," Mr. Hardy offered.

The lady twisted her hands in front of her. "What I am about to tell you, we never shared with Sara for her own safety. We never wanted her to learn about our connection to her grandmother because of the danger it placed her in. But when she started visiting our shoppe, we agreed it was our mission to protect her the best we could. That is why we offered her refuge when she lost her position with Lord Baldridge. We encouraged her to take the position in Scotland because it would keep Lord and Lady Roselli from learning who she was."

Somerville frowned. "How are you connected to my wife?"

Mr. Hardy rested his hand on his wife's shoulder. "Her grandmother was my sister."

Somerville leaned back in the chair. "Then you understand what danger Sara is in."

Mrs. Hardy squeezed her husband's hand. "Yes, we understand. That is why we warned her away. Her grandmother wrote to us about Sara's birth and the consequences of keeping her. My husband paid for her to hide away in Fordwich while she raised Sara. When we learned of her passing, we had no clue what had happened to Sara. When she walked into our bookshop, we thought it was a miracle. Now we fear we have placed her in danger."

"Nay. You have nothing to do with the danger surrounding Sara. That is her misfortunate of being the child of Lord and Lady Roselli. What I do not understand is how Lord Roselli learned the connection between Sara and you?" Somerville questioned.

"I fear that lies with me. I warned the bastard to never step foot in my shoppe when he first started visiting earlier last year before Sara left for Scotland," Mr. Hardy answered.

"How did that incident strike his curiosity?" Somerville wondered aloud.

"He noticed Sara and inquired about her. She insisted on assisting in the shoppe to earn her keep while she stayed with us. You must understand that Sara is the spitting image of her mother in her youth," Mrs. Hardy explained.

"I must stop Lord Roselli from finding her. He has tormented Sara and her friends this past year. I fear how he might harm her to protect his image."

"Her grandmother's cottage is the place she would run to," Mr. Hardy guessed.

Sommerville rose and offered his hand in gratitude. "Thank you for your help, and I apologize for my discourteous behavior."

Mr. Hardy shook Somerville's hand. "Please find our niece."

"I intend to."

Chapter Eighteen

False Rumors

Sara awoke to a crackling fire and a blanket thrown over her. In her muddled state of wakefulness, she neglected to notice she wasn't alone. She sat up and glanced around the cottage, and to her horror, she noticed Lord and Lady Roselli had made themselves at home. They sat across from her with a pot of tea in between them on a stand.

"Ahh, look, my dear, our daughter has risen from her nap," Lord Roselli drawled.

"I see, my darling. However, she still looks a bit peaked." Lady Roselli sipped at her tea.

"Then perhaps you should offer her some relief. She must be parched after her long carriage ride. After all, you are playing hostess of this lovely cottage."

Sara bristled at Lord Roselli's sarcasm. She refused to refer to him as her father. Silence was her weapon of choice. She wouldn't give them any ammunition to strike against her. She refused to ask them why they terrorized her because they would only spew lies to defend their actions.

It didn't even matter. She'd had her grandmother's love growing up and got to experience the greatest love with Ian. Not to mention, Mairi gifted her with the love of a child. Even her friends offered her the love of a sister with their friendship. Lord and Lady Roselli's vendetta would fail once they realized she didn't care about them. Her feelings didn't differ from the treatment she received from them since her birth.

"Well, I must be. Our daughter has disappointed us with her ungracious manners. And to believe she is a duchess, no less," Lady Roselli murmured while pouring Sara a cup of tea.

Sara sat up straight with her hands in her lap. She wouldn't allow them to belittle her with their petty comments. Somerville had shown her that her confidence was her greatest weapon, and she would use it to defend herself against them. Being a parent now, she couldn't believe the travesty against her to have these degenerate souls as her parents.

"Drink the tea your mother prepared for you," Lord Roselli ordered.

The cup remained untouched, and her defiance rang clear. However, her disobedience struck a nerve with Lord Roselli. He pounded his fist on the table. His fury rattled her to pick up the cup. However, she refused to drink the tea.

"Now," his thunderous tone demanded.

Sara lifted the cup to her mouth and swallowed the bitter liquid. When she lowered the cup to the table, the victorious smile Lord Roselli gave her sent a shiver racing along her spine. It was then that Sara realized she was at their mercy, no matter how brave she pretended to be.

Lord Roselli inclined his head. "Thank you."

Sara stayed quiet, her thoughts racing at how she could escape from their clutches. Even though they hadn't tied her up, she was at a disadvantage to protect herself. Her only option was to cause conflict between them. She thought to plea to Lady Roselli's motherly instincts. Until she remembered the lady had ordered Sara's grandmother to dispose of Sara after she gave birth. They'd spent Sara's lifetime covering their tracks. She would find no success in dissuading either of them.

Lord Roselli folded his hands and pressed his fingers against his lips as he observed her. "My darling Sara. We have a dilemma that needs resolved with undo haste." He turned to glare at his wife. "One my wife should have resolved years ago." He focused his attention back on Sara. "However, now it is a necessity. You must understand how it is nothing personal. However, we cannot have you converting around in society. You draw too much attention to a past we have kept hidden from our peers. Your appearance last year placed us in a dilemma we cannot be in. Our only option is your death."

"I am leaving England and Scotland. You have nothing to worry about," Sara interrupted.

Lady Roselli placed her hand over her heart. "Oh, dear, 'tis never that simple. The duke will not allow you to disappear without a fight. His search will become relentless to return you to his side."

Sara shook her head. "I will write him a letter to convince him otherwise."

"If only it were as straightforward as you propose. However, his actions have already proven otherwise. Now we must decide. Should we end your life now or wait for Somerville's arrival so he can perish along with you?" Lord Roselli mused.

"No!"

Lord Roselli shook his head at Sara's display of anguish. "You have no choice in this decision. However, my wife explained why we must keep the duke alive. We are doing him a service by killing you. Especially since his duchess stated her deceit for all the ton to hear. No one would question your death. But if we killed the duke, it would place us under the ton's scrutiny. Somerville's influential friends would make it their mission to pin his death on us. Your fiery death in a cottage would draw sympathy to the duke. Until he became the primary suspect in your death to hide his shame of making you his duchess."

Lady Roselli clapped her hands. "You are brilliant as always, my love." She smiled at Sara as if they were discussing fabric for a new dress. "A fire was how we rid ourselves of his first wife."

"Ah, yes, the tragic death of my first wife gave me the brilliant idea."

Sara had sworn she wouldn't ask them the reason for their cruelty, but she needed to understand the depth of their depravity if she had any chance of escaping. "Why?"

"Simple, my dear. We never wanted you. When your grandmother defied your mother's request, it left an unwanted obstacle in our path. We thought we were in the clear when my first wife's death didn't draw any speculation about our affair. However, our circle of friends learned about your mother's unwanted pregnancy. So your mother left to quiet the rumors. In the meantime, my wife died in a tragic fire at our estate. Your mother was to end her pregnancy. However, I learned of her deception when I had her followed. When your grandmother escaped with you, we made the mistake of letting her leave. We thought she would stay hidden and keep our secret of who your parents were. So your mother returned to London, sympathetic to the death of my wife, and soon society accepted her into their fold."

Lord Roselli paused as he rose from his seat. "We never planned for your grandmother's death. Your arrival in London caught us by surprise. We thought your banishment to Scotland would solve our problems. But your association with those other social climbers made us realize your demise was our only saving grace. Threatening your friends was useless. Our only option was to destroy you instead. If you cannot understand our predicament, 'tis simple. Anyone who crosses our path will find their demise at our hands."

Sara stared at them. "Have you no kindness in your souls?"

Lady Roselli cackled. "Kindness is for fools. If you have not realized, life is not kind, my dear. It will not offer you the salvation you so desire. Life is about taking care of oneself."

It was difficult to understand how these two individuals were her parents. They didn't even deserve the title. They were the devil and his mistress in disguise. Sara hoped Ian would strike his vengeance and see them destroyed. They would meet their maker one day and get what they deserved.

A chill overtook Sara, and she wrapped herself in the blanket. She lifted her head when Lord and Lady Roselli pulled on their coats. But her eyes grew heavy, and she fought to keep them open. Even then, she had trouble seeing them through her blurry vision. She raised her hand to wipe her eyes but to no avail. The couple doubled before her.

"It would appear the sleeping potion has taken effect. Do not fight it. We are not cruel. We have no wish for you to suffer through the fire that will claim your life. You will not feel a thing as the flames lick away at your body," Lord Roselli explained.

Lady Roselli tugged on her gloves. "Contrary to our actions, it has been a pleasure to make your acquaintance, dear Sara."

Sara closed her eyes and mumbled an incoherent response. She couldn't return the sentiment. Nor could she fight her fate. They had taken that option away from her. She didn't want to focus her last thought on them. She wanted to remember Ian's loving smile as he wrapped her in his embrace, kissing her with the passion they shared. And Mairi's sweet voice calling her Momma as they held hands and read a story. She fell back against the cushions, unable to save herself.

Her life was but a memory.

False Rumors

Ian clutched Sara's hand, praying for her to awaken. It had been two days since he rescued her from the fire at her grandmother's cottage. The doctor explained the trauma she'd suffered kept her in a deep sleep. However, he worried it was something more tragic than that. He feared she would never recover from the effects of the smoke. He refused to leave her side in case she met her demise.

Ian raged at the injustice his wife suffered at the hands of her selfish parents. But they had met their demise in their attempt to escape their cruelty. Their deaths in a carriage accident was a blessing. However, the nightmare continued with Sara's injuries. If only she would wake and smile at him. Only then would everything be all right.

He kissed her knuckles. "You are safe, my love."

The horror he'd met when he arrived in Fordwich still plagued him every second she never returned to him. He'd thought he'd lost her as flames licked at the cottage. Without his friends' help, he would've lost Sara forever. Lockhart and Courtland had kicked the door down, while Hepburn had doused their clothing with water from the pump and helped him search for Sara. They'd found her on the settee, wrapped in a blanket. Ian had lifted her and carried her to safety. Her labored breathing had been a welcomed sign of her survival.

The local physician had checked her over and informed him the smoke she'd inhaled might cause her death. He had no remedy to offer, other than to make Sara comfortable. Only time would be their answer. He'd raced her back to London for another opinion, only for his physicians to tell him the same. His frustration mounted every second she never awakened. The only justice was when his friends delivered the news of Lord and Lady Rosellis' deaths. Sara was now free from their terror.

He slid beneath the sheets and gathered Sara into his arms. Like the past two nights, he hoped his warmth would revive her. He fought against falling asleep, but exhaustion took hold. Ian tightened his embrace to hold Sara closer while he succumbed to sleep.

He prayed their nightmare would end when he awoke.

False Rumors

Sara struggled to lift her eyelids. Nor did she wish for her dream to end with Ian holding her close to his heart. However, the terror of what awaited her had her wrenching from the hold that kept her asleep. She jolted to a sitting position, struggling to catch her breath as her gaze darted around. The familiar sight of the bedchamber she shared with Ian greeted her, along with the faint light of the sun shining through the windows.

The last thing she remembered was her parents laughing in delight at her imminent death. Terror shook her frame as flashes of their cruelty demanded her attention. They meant for her to die in a fire, the same fate her father's first wife had met. A lady who was an innocent victim married to a degenerate who cared less about her welfare. The same treatment Sara had endured at her parents' selfish expense.

As Sara calmed down, she realized she hadn't been dreaming. Ian had held her in a loving embrace. Her dear husband appeared distressed, if his appearance reflected his agony. Guilt racked her for how she had left him. She'd never meant to cause him any suffering. His love for her was greater than anything she had ever imagined.

He lay on the pillow facing her with a few days' worth of whiskers. He was never one to leave their bedchamber without a shave. His hair lay in a tousled mess, and he slept in his clothes.

Sara placed her hand on his cheek and whispered, "Ian?"

Ian jerked awake at Sara's scratchy voice. "Sara!"

Sara rubbed her throat. "What happened?"

He pulled her close, unable to answer her. The shock of seeing her awake overwhelmed him. Tears streamed down his face. He kissed the top of her head and then showered her face with kisses. "Do not speak, my love. Your throat needs to heal from the smoke you inhaled."

"The fire," Sara squeaked.

"Yes."

Ian's tears prompted her own to fall as Sara realized how precious the love they'd almost lost was. "My hero."

Ian shook his head in refusal. He played no hero, only a husband who was desperate to save the woman he loved. However, he had failed on all accounts to keep her safe. If he had been vigilant in Sara's protection, then he never would've had to rescue her from a fiery cottage.

Sara noticed how Ian blamed himself for the predicament he'd rescued her from. "Not your fault."

"Shh, rest, my love. We will talk once you have recovered."

Ian pressed Sara's head against his chest. He couldn't bear to stare into her eyes and know she considered him a hero, not while he fought the guilt of placing her in danger. As her husband he only wanted to show Sara how much he treasured her. However, he'd failed. Because of her insecurities and how she doubted the depth of his love, she'd run away to protect him, when he should've been the one protecting her.

His hand coasted along her hair in a soothing gesture of affection. Soon, her grip on his shirt loosened as she fell back asleep. He must come to terms with his guilt if their marriage had any chance to survive. Sara deserved a husband worthy of her love.

A gentleman he hoped to be one day.

Chapter Nineteen

False Rumors

Ian lifted Mairi off Sara's lap. "Tell your momma good night."

Mairi wrapped her tiny arms around Sara's neck and clung tightly. "Night, Momma."

Sara's ordeal had frightened Mairi. Sara made every attempt to reassure her daughter of her love. She couldn't make promises out of her control, but she could make it possible to never leave her again on purpose.

Sara returned her hug and kissed her on the cheek. "Night, my love. We will continue your story tomorrow."

Ian brushed his lips across Sara's. "I will return shortly."

His presence soothed Sara's frayed emotions. Ever since she awakened three days ago, he had never left her for long and always showered her with loving attention. They had yet to discuss the impact of her ordeal, and Sara decided they would this evening. She needed to put the past behind her so she could enjoy her future with Ian. Too many doubts lingered between them that they needed to discuss. Only then would their nightmare be over.

Sara rose from the bed Ian had ordered her to stay in. She wrapped her robe around her and moved to wait for Ian on the settee. Her change in position would force him to acknowledge their need to talk. If he refused, then Sara wouldn't hesitate to remind him of the passion between them. His time treating her with precious care would end this evening. She wasn't a fragile miss but a brave duchess.

"She wanted to sleep with us again. We should never have allowed her to," Ian said as he entered the suite.

"It helped to soothe her fears," Sara disagreed.

Ian stopped and swung his gaze from the bed to where his wife rested on the settee. "You need to be in bed."

Sara narrowed her gaze at his high-handed demand. "I need for you to join me." She held out her hand.

The determination in his wife's eyes showed him they would have their long-awaited discussion that evening. He came to her side and clasped her hand before lowering himself next to her. If they were to discuss her near-death experience, then he wanted her wrapped in his loving embrace.

"I am sorry to have worried you and Mairi when I fled," Sara started.

"Why did you?"

"I overheard you speaking with Marian and Stuart about attending an event. You argued with them, and Marian expressed her distaste for my recent behavior. My greatest fear had come true of shaming your family. I thought it would be best if I left. When I read the letter from my father, my only thought was to protect you and Mairi," Sara admitted.

Ian tipped her chin up. "Ah, love, you misunderstood. Marian wasn't ashamed of you. She had grown concerned about how the strain of your father's terror affected you. I had been blind to your misery in my attempt to keep you safe. In which I failed. If you had felt secure in my love, you would have shared your fears with me."

The unconventional start to their marriage had left them both unsure of the other's feelings. Even after confessing their love, their doubts had lingered. Doubts Sara no longer held and she hoped Ian felt the same.

"I was a fool to ever doubt our love. Can you ever forgive me?"

Ian brushed the hair from Sara's eyes. "There is nothing to forgive, my love. You are here and safe in my arms, where I hope you will always remain."

"I promise," Sara pledged with a kiss.

Ian sank back into the cushions, pulling Sara with him. "After you have recovered, I wish to return to Scotland if you agree."

"I wish for nothing more."

Ian tightened his embrace before broaching the delicacy of the next topic of conversation. They had spoken of nothing but their love for one another since he rescued her. However, they'd never discussed the torment she'd endured at her parents' hands. He didn't wish for her to recall the events, but he hoped it would help with her recovery.

"I am here for you whenever you wish to discuss your ordeal."

Sara turned into Ian's arms and stared deeply into his eyes. She noted his hesitation in asking her about her torment. She never wanted to relive those moments. However, if she were to heal, then she must confide in Ian the terrors that plagued her whenever she was alone.

Sara told Ian of the trauma she'd endured with an ease she never expected. The comfort of his arms reassured her that her parents could never harm her again. However, when she came to the part concerning her parents' cruelty, she had to pause while tears flooded her with the terror and grief she'd experienced. Throughout it all, Ian remained steadfast with his love and support.

They discussed long into the night her feelings about her parents' and grandmother's secrets. Ian explained how the Hardys were her aunt and uncle and how they wished for a relationship with her if she was amicable to one. Ian explained how he'd rescued her with their friends' help. He shared his grief of waiting for her to return to him. Sara never wanted either of them to experience the terror they'd endured ever again.

"Know this, my dear Sara, you are loved by everyone. By me especially. Never allow your parents' cruelty to leave doubts about how very special you are to all those who love you."

Sara smiled at him with the same tender smile he had fallen in love with. His wife was a treasure he would guard with his heart. He never thought he would love again. Especially not a love that left him shaken. However, Sara proved miracles happened.

Ian's declaration warmed Sara's heart. His love was a precious reminder of the fragileness of life, but also one that proved one must endure hardship to enjoy the simplicity of another's love. Ian's love was her salvation she would cherish forever.

"I love you, my darling husband."

Ian rose with Sara in his arms and carried her to their bed. He slid them between the sheets and kissed her with the softest of kisses. "I love you, my darling wife."

Sara sighed into Ian's kiss as he caressed her with his loving touch. She had ached for his touch the past few days. While he never left her side, he had kept himself at a distance, as if he might break her. Now he showed her his distance was only his act as a gentleman to allow her time to recover. His touch set her desire aflame with a need only he could fulfill.

His lips trailed a path of fire along her body as he slid her nightdress off. Sara arched into his touch, her body begging him to possess her. She'd thought she would never experience Ian's lovemaking again when she left. Now the power of their connection was so profound, Sara moaned at the effect it held over her.

She held his head to her chest as he suckled at her breasts. However, when he parted her thighs and slid his fingers into her pussy, Sara could no longer hold back from expressing the relief he brought from his touch alone.

"Ian."

Sara's breathy moan urged Ian to savor her sweetness on his tongue. He slid between her thighs and dipped his head to blow a soft breath against her core. Her wetness glistened from her desire. A desire he hungered to explore with one delicious lick after another. At the first stroke of his tongue across her decadent pussy, Ian lost himself in Sara's whimpers of pleasure. He swirled a path between her folds, savoring her essence.

When Sara tightened her hold on his hair and arched her hips in rhythm with his fingers, he devoured her wetness with a relentless hunger that would take him forever to satisfy. Her clit hardened under his attention with the swift flicks of his tongue, drawing her toward the edge. Sara's thighs pressed against his head, holding him hostage to ensure her pleasure.

Ian inhaled the musk of her desire, losing himself in Sara's scent. He was a husband desperate for his wife to explode on his tongue. He slid his hand along her body and pinched her nipple between his fingers, twisting with a desperate urgency to send her flying.

"Ian."

Ian's attention had her swirling in the whirlwind of their love. She abandoned control, losing herself in Ian's passionate touch. Her body shook from the orgasm that ripped through her. Nothing compared to how Ian loved her with his heart and soul. She had lost her heart to him the second she met him.

Before she could recover from the onslaught of Ian's passion, he entered her with such slow precision that Sara was positive her heart had stopped beating. But as soon as he sank in as deep as he could and she wrapped herself around him, her heart started beating again, a slow rhythm that matched their bodies moving as one. It was a dance as old as time. They moved against one another, with their bodies pressed close to feel the other's heartbeat.

Ian entwined their fingers together and pressed a soft kiss to Sara's lips. "You are the other half of my soul, and I love you with all my heart."

Tears slipped from Sara's eyes at Ian's gentle lovemaking and the love shining from his eyes. "My heart only beats for you, and I will love you for an eternity and beyond."

Their love was a rare gem that neither of them had ever expected, one that had flourished out of their control into something they would never take for granted. They were two lost souls who had found one another when they thought they were alone. A stroke of luck, some would say.

However, destiny would disagree.

Epilogue

False Rumors

SARA STARED ACROSS THE lawn of the park at her husband, who carried Mairi on his shoulders. She could watch the two of them endlessly. The special bond they shared was a delight to admire. Ian was an amazing father who indulged his daughter every chance he got. He was also an amazing husband too. Sara found no fault with him in the slightest.

After she recovered from her injuries, they had left London behind for their home in Edinburgh. Ian promised they would spend the summer traveling to his other estates throughout Scotland. The thought of his vast estates would've frightened her before, but with Ian by her side, she was eager to visit them.

Before she left, she'd visited the Hardys, and they had corresponded with each other weekly since her return to Scotland. Ian had invited them for a visit in the fall, and they had agreed. Her parents had never wanted her, but she'd found a family that welcomed her with open arms. She embraced the relationship with happiness.

As for her parents, Sara never gave them any consideration. They had never factored into her life before. The terror they'd inflicted on her and her friends was all the more reason to forget they had even existed. To consider the damage they'd caused only gave them power in death. Sara had resolved herself to deny them any influence in her life.

Only joyous thoughts kept her grounded.

"It is so adorable how she still blushes when she stares at him," Flora teased.

Sara's lips lifted in a secretive smile. If her friends only knew why she blushed when she stared at her husband, they would blush too. "Mmm," she murmured.

"I, for one, find their love charming to watch," Grace mused.

"A love affair to admire," Vivian agreed.

Sara turned to Vivian. "One I must thank you for."

Vivian frowned. "How so?"

"If not for your urgings for us to start anew in Scotland, I never would have met Ian. Because of you, I found love and a family," Sara explained.

Vivian smiled. "You are a wonderful mother to Mairi."

Sara hugged Vivian. "Not only Mairi and Ian but you ladies are the sisters I never had. I cherish your friendship and the sense of family we have become."

Grace and Flora joined their hug, expressing their agreement. They had crossed many obstacles in the journey of their friendship, but through it all, they had remained steadfast in their love and support. When she lost her grandmother, Sara had never felt more alone. However, on a chance meeting one day in the park, she'd found more than she ever imagined by stepping out of her shell of loneliness and embracing the comforting warmth of friendship. Without these ladies in her life, Sara would find herself lost. The false rumors spread about them had only strengthened their bond.

"I beg your pardon. I need to steal my wife for a spell," Ian interrupted them.

"Spell, more like the rest of the afternoon." Flora snickered.

Ian winked at Flora. "Perhaps."

Grace waved them away. "You can take her now, but during our next visit, we need her to ourselves."

Ian bowed to them. "I shall accommodate your wishes."

Sara giggled at Ian's silliness. A year ago, her husband had been a prim and proper duke. However, with each day, more of his true character showed.

Ian's reserved behavior had resulted from his grieving for his first wife and the terror he tried to protect Sara from. Now, with their life free of worries, her husband lived life to the fullest with a happiness she loved to enjoy.

Ian tucked Sara to his side as he led her to the carriage. She glanced over her shoulder at Mairi playing with her friends. "Are we not forgetting someone?"

Ian followed Sara's gaze, then looked forward again. "No. I have everyone I need for my afternoon plans."

Sara frowned at him. "Our daughter?"

Ian lifted Sara into the carriage and settled next to her before pulling her onto his lap. "I do not believe we can tell this early. Or can we?"

Sara's eyes widened. "You ... How ..."

Ian chuckled. "My love, I thought we agreed on no more secrets."

Sara swatted his hands as he tried to tug off her coat. "You ruined my surprise."

Ian kissed along her neck as his hand skated up her skirts to caress her legs. "Surprise? Mmm. I enjoy the sound of that much better."

Sara's eyes lowered as she arched her neck to give him better access. "Mairi?"

"Mairi is spending the afternoon with her friends. Grace promised to care for her while we spend the day together celebrating our surprise."

Sara wrapped her arms around Ian's neck and drew him toward her for a kiss. "Have I told you today how I am the luckiest duchess ever?"

Ian sighed into Sara's kiss. "Then I guess that makes me the luckiest duke ever."

Luck didn't even begin to describe their grand love.

False Rumors

Hello Lovely Readers,

Thank you for reading my governess series False Rumors. I hope you've enjoyed falling in love with the characters as much as I've loved writing them.

Now onto my next project ...

Happy Reading!

Laura

"Thank you for reading The Honorable Governess. Gaining exposure as an independent author relies mostly on word-of-mouth, so if you have the time and inclination, please consider leaving a short review wherever you can."

Want to join my mailing list? Visit www.lauraabarnes.com today!

Desire other books to read by Laura A. Barnes

Enjoy these other romance books:

Historical Romances

<u>False Rumors Series</u>

The Fallen Governess

The Wishful Governess

The Secretive Governess

The Honorable Governess

<u>Fate of the Worthingtons Series</u>

The Tempting Minx

The Seductive Temptress
The Fiery Vixen
The Siren's Gentleman

Matchmaking Madness Series

How the Lady Charmed the Marquess
How the Earl Fell for His Countess
How the Rake Tempted the Lady
How the Scot Stole the Bride
How the Lady Seduced the Viscount
How the Lord Married His Lady

Tricking the Scoundrels Series:

Whom Shall I Kiss... An Earl, A Marquess, or A Duke?
Whom Shall I Marry... An Earl or A Duke?
I Shall Love the Earl
The Scoundrel's Wager
The Forgiven Scoundrel

Romancing the Spies Series:

Rescued By the Captain
Rescued By the Spy
Rescued By the Scot
Romancing the Spies Collection Box Set

Contemporary Romances

Mitchell Winery Series:

Seduced by Fate
Seduced by Temptation
Seduced by Destiny

About Author Laura A. Barnes

International bestselling author Laura A. Barnes fell in love with writing in the second grade. After her first creative writing assignment, she dreamt of becoming an author. Many years went by with Laura filling her head full of story ideas and some funny fish songs she wrote while fishing with her family. In 2017, she made her dreams a reality. With her debut novel Rescued By the Captain, she has set out on the path of a published author.

When not writing, Laura can be found devouring her favorite romance books. Laura is married to her own Prince Charming (who for some reason or another thinks the heroes in her books are about him) who she enjoys traveling with and binging shows on streaming services. You can usually find her spending time with her children and grandchildren. Besides her love of reading and writing, Laura loves to travel. With her passport stamped in England, Scotland, and Ireland; she hopes to add more countries to her list soon.

While Laura isn't very good on the social media front, she loves to hear from her readers. You can find her on the following platforms:

You can visit her at ***www.lauraabarnes.com*** to join her mailing list.

Website: https://www.lauraabarnes.com/

Amazon: https://amazon.com/author/lauraabarnes

Goodreads: https://www.goodreads.com/author/show/16332844.Laura_A_Barnes

Facebook: https://www.facebook.com/AuthorLauraA.Barnes/

Instagram: https://www.instagram.com/labarnesauthor/

Twitter: https://twitter.com/labarnesauthor

BookBub: https://www.bookbub.com/profile/laura-a-barnes

TikTok: https://www.tiktok.com/@labarnesauthor

www.ingramcontent.com/pod-product-compliance
Ingram Content Group UK Ltd.
Pitfield, Milton Keynes, MK11 3LW, UK
UKHW040639180225
455202UK00001B/110

9 798227 734785